VOLUME FOUR
SHORT BITS

FIVE ORIGINAL SCIENCE
FICTION & FANTASY STORIES

BELINDA CRAWFORD

HENDRIX & FAUST
PUBLISHERS

Books by Belinda Crawford

The Hero Rebellion
(Hunter)
Hero
(Race)
Riven
Regan

The Echo
Cold Between Stars
Dark Between Oceans
Echo Between Worlds
(Brother)

Demons & Battleskirts
Volume 1

Collections
Short Bits Volume 1
Short Bits Volume 2
Short Bits Volume 3
Short Bits Volume 4

CONTENTS

Introduction 7

Transmission 9

Corpses & Demons Horses 31

Felis Fetura 39

Letters I'll Never Send.................................... 65

Dread Space... 93

INTRODUCTION

Did you know that this volume of *Short Bits* marks two years of me publishing this collection? It seems kind of amazing, but also not that long ago, and yet... Two years is seven hundred and thirty days and that's... huge!

I was super nervous publishing *Short Bits Volume 1*, not quite sure if what I was writing could actually be classified as short stories or were just random bits without proper beginnings or endings. Now... I'm more confident and I'm really, *really* enjoying writing these shorts.

I hope you enjoy reading them just as much. :)

This collection has a strong sci-fi bent, with a little bit of weird thrown in for good measure. You'll also notice a certain Asiatic twist to a few of the stories, which I attribute to my addiction to East Asian storytelling (also Bollywood, although the random dance numbers take a little getting used to).

Happy reading,
Belinda

TRANSMISSION

INTRODUCTION

On the back wall of my office, is a very long timeline mapping out all the stories in my science-fiction universe. It starts from the year 2000 and goes all the way to 3350, and only ends there because there's a story idea (working title, 'Terramancer') at 3031 that I haven't dipped my toe into yet. I figure the timeline will expand once I write that.

I think the thing I'm enjoying most about writing these short stories is how it lets me fill out the timeline in little chunks; adding colour to the universe and influencing the tales that follow. Although the characters in one series probably won't pop up in another, the events that take place, and the technology they're using, tend to build on each other.

Transmission takes place around the year 2854, between *SEED* (which appeared in *Short Bits Volume 3*) and 'Terramancer'. While *Transmission* doesn't directly influence what I *think* 'Terramancer' is going to be about, it adds that "almost magic" spin to the technology that'll appear in later stories.

Learn more about the writing of *Transmission*.
Scan the QR code for the audio commentary.

TRANSMISSION

Blood painted the bulkhead in giant arcs of red flung from the curve of her sword. She slashed again, black nano-steel slicing through flesh and bone, warm arterial spray slicking her face even as the ImpMit's head thumped on the deck.

The soldier's body still stood, the pale grey slabs of its power-armoured legs holding it upright. A swift kick to the back of the knee had it tumbling to join its fellows on the deck, and it was done.

For the moment, at least.

Du'ata paused, sword extended, her weight balanced. The long, bum-sweeping tail of her ink-dark braid had come loose during the fight, and her red and teal outer robe, with its rich gold embroidery was dark with blood, but the slick black nano-armour underneath remained intact. No warnings popped on her mask's HUD, nothing save the empty corridor and the pulsing emergency lights.

She breathed deep, taking in the stench of death-loosened bowls, the copper tang of blood sweet on the back of her tongue, and listened. To the rush of her heart, the sigh of the air-cyclers, and that giant empty nothingness that came from soundproofed bulkheads and the absence of living souls.

Just the square, pale-grey walls of the ImpMit cruiser, emergency lights flashing orange along the join of wall and floor. The holoscreens that usually lined the walls were gone, the emitters at either end sparking electricity, the surveillance cams little more than evenly spaced scorch marks, victims of her pistol in that initial rush, the hectic dance to jam the bulkheads.

The round-cornered hatches at either end of the ten-metre section of corridor flashed more eye-searing orange, another reminder of the disaster happening in their midst. The corpses at her feet.

A sharp flick sent loose blood flying from her blade—more red to decorate the walls—before she slid it into the sheath at her hip, the nano-steel singing as it found home.

Her HUD flashed, another screen overlaying her vision as new targets appeared behind her. She turned, fatigue dragging at her bones, the internal chem-pharm that had kept her going this long, now depleted. No more adrenaline, no more stims, not until they got off this boat.

If they got off this boat.

Her HUD flashed again, the new targets closing in. The threat not immediate but close.

A twitch of her eye and the map expanded, new dots—one brilliant green, the other two gold—popped up. Too close. Everything and everyone was too close.

She swore and popped the comms. 'Get them out, Rehc.'

On the HUD, the green dot didn't change, but she could see Rehc's snarl, teeth a sharp slash of white in his black face. 'Trying,' he said, his voice a growl, strain giving it an extra rumble.

She didn't say 'try harder', although the words hovered on the back of her tongue as she watched the enemy advance, their scarlet dots flowing through the ship's corridors. Rehc would get the Lady and her daughter out or live long enough to make sure they didn't suffer at the Empire's hands. Which would be longer than her, if the emergency hatch didn't hold.

It wouldn't hold of course, not forever, but she didn't need forever, she just needed enough time—

The hatch blew inwards.

She had time to see it bow, to appreciate the inch-thick steelcrete, how the explosive hadn't just blackened the edges but eaten at them too, and to curse herself for not thinking the ImpMits would be able to fool her radar, before she was slammed into a bulkhead.

Pain swamped her chest, hot and burning. Even as her internals screamed, catastrophic med warnings exploded across her HUD, telling of punctured lungs and shattered ribs, while novas burst in her vision. The world was a brilliant explosion of colour as her internals stuttered, trying desperately to fix a failing body, short-circuiting eyes and ears, leaving instinct and training to take over from conscious decision.

Her hand found her sword, nanite-infused blood spilling down the hilt, energising the blade, shredding the scabbard.

The ImpMits coming through the blown door—black clad and faceless—were blurred shadows in her eyes, but she found one. Lunged. Struck, blade sinking into flesh—

Time stuttered. Elastic. Sticky.

Fragmented.

She was on the deck, sensors guiding hands that felt alien, closing too-long fingers over a gun, the stock meeting her shoulder even as the weapon hummed and fired.

Stars still glazed her vision, whited-out the details of face and form, but the HUD took over for her visual cortex and guided her aim. One red dot down. Two.

Heat signatures blazed then fell. More poured in after them, and more and more and more. More than there should be, more than there *could* be. They were all blending together, no longer neat outlines of colour but an amorphous mass of red and yellow.

She needed her eyes, Terra damn it. Needed her eyes! But the blow to her head and… and something, something she should remember, clouded her vision.

She shook her head, trying to dislodge the white.

Breath on her neck, a blade, cold and sharp against her throat.

Her fingers jammed on the trigger.

'Hello, Du'ata.'

Her blood went cold.

—

Time fragmented again.

There was no feeling in her legs, her arms, the limbs had long since turned to ice, the thin grey jumpsuit no match for her frigid cell. Her hands and feet were blocky, the muscles she could still feel—abdomen and neck and shoulders—beyond her ability to command. Not even her head responded, her lips or cheeks or eyes, though she felt them, felt the chill brush of air, the warmth of the light playing across her eyelids, caressing her lips. She'd felt, too, the hands that slipped under her, the arms that lifted her off the hard, cold cot, the tendons in her neck pulling as her head flopped back.

Heavy boots clomped on the plassteel deck, the sound louder now than before, with her weight adding to the force, ringing off the dark walls of her cell. A door *swooshed*, a command panel *beeped*, and the body carrying her paused, the hands wrapped around her bicep and hip gripping tighter before it moved again. Another *swoosh*. The jolt of short, steady strides, boots no longer echoing off hard cell walls, but still tension moving through the arms holding her.

Was that anxiety that radiated through the not-cold arm brushing against her cheek? Who on an ImpMit cruiser would be anxious with her, a half-dead Shar warrior, in their arms? Who would carry her? Why not a med-slab or a body bag? Was that the cross-hatched roughness of nanoarmour through her jumpsuit? The cold ridges of powered-arms pressing into her back? The butt of a gun nudging her ribs?

Questions raced through her brain, made her eyes flicker behind stubbornly closed lids.

Cherry blossom teased her nose, the sweet scent reminding

her... Of what? She couldn't remember. Why couldn't she remember? There was a black hole in the middle of her brain, a space where something important... no someone important, and the smell, the blossoms teased that spot, made it snap and crackle and—

'We're almost there.' The chest next to her ear rumbled with the words, the sound of them soft, almost lost under the steady clang of boots on deck. The steady feminine voice was familiar, in the way the scent was familiar, ringing that bell in the darkness, making lightning arch between neurons, the electric tang of them thick on her tongue.

Was the woman speaking to her? Did she know Du'ata was aware within her broken shell, that she longed to move her lips, to twitch her eyelashes? That she would give anything, anything at all, for a sharp blade and the strength to slide it between her ribs? Did she? Would she?

'Have the med-pod ready.'

No, those words were not for her. The woman spoke to another, her words not quite a whisper. And with those words, the quiet undertone designed to disappear under the ringing tang of her boots, she gave herself away. She was not an ImpMit, not one of the hard-faced soldiers or dead-eyed inquisitors who had broken Du'ata's bones, torn her tendons, shredded her mind.

'It's bad.' A pause, seconds marked by boots clanking on the deck once more, the gentle bounce of her head with each of the woman's strides. 'Yes,' she said again, short, to the point.

Another pause. 'I don't know.'

What didn't the woman know? What didn't Du'ata know? Why was there a hole in her mind? Was it the torture? The endless, hellish interrogations, the probes jacked into her greyware, the drugs pumped into her chem-pharm? But no, the hole felt deeper than that, older, the edges precise where the inquisitor's had been ragged and rough.

New sounds; the distant hum of multiple conversations, the

gentle beep and squark of consoles, the almost inaudible growl of massive engines vibrating through equally massive bulkheads.

'We're at the hangar. Get ready.'

Another door shushing open and now the smell of grease and oil assaulted her nose, and the squark and beep was taken over by the ear-ringing clang of metal on metal and the brain-piercing whine of drills. All of it echoing and echoing and echoing. The cacophony swallowed the sound of the woman's footfalls, her quiet whispers, but her voice travelled through her chest and rumbled against Du'ata's side.

New lights played over her eyelids, no longer warm yellow but sharp and red, the intermittent pulses driving nails into what was left of her brain. Pain spread under her skull, and she couldn't help the moan that rose from her chest.

The woman paused, little more than a momentary hesitation, and her hands tightened on Du'ata's shoulder and leg. Was that a curse she felt rumbling through the woman's chest, did her footsteps hasten? Did—

'Hey! You! Stop!' Those words exploded over the cacophony, coming from behind.

The woman didn't stop, didn't turn either. She shifted her grip, muscles moving under nanoarmour, and then Du'ata was over the woman's shoulder and the woman was running, breath expelling from Du'ata's lungs with every deck-eating stride.

Gunfire. She felt it as much as heard it. The razor burn of it ripping past her cheek, the forward stagger of the woman, the *phzt stick*, the heady metallic taste of burned ozone.

A whine deep enough to squeeze the very air and then—

A supernova bloomed, a giant wave of heat and light washing away sound and colour, everything save the shoulder robbing her of air, the skull-splitting bounce as the woman pounded the deck.

There were other noises, lost under the ringing in her ears, the stars behind her unresponsive lids. Light turned to dark, heat to cold, the hiss and snick of an airlock cycling closed. The supernova gone as quickly as it came and then the shoulder was gone from her stomach, air rushed into her lungs and for a moment, a second, her eyelids parted—

Her own drawn, ghastly ivory face reflected in a shiny black mask, hollow cheeks and cracked lips, eyes bruised and sunken. And then there were more people, forms she saw on the edge of her vision, shapes caught just like her reflection in the woman's obliterating mask.

And underneath that... The rumble of engines, a sudden lurch as the deck heaved under them. She knew those sounds. Knew the stomach-hollowing jerk, recognised the woman's quick shuffle as the actions of an emergency take-off in hostile surrounds before the inertial dampeners could kick in.

Another lurch but the woman barely staggered, striding down the ship's corridor, the forms in her mask keeping pace. 'She's awake,' she said, no hint of strain in her voice, none of the tension radiating through her arms.

A soft curse, familiar as the woman's was familiar, and though she struggled to identify it, to chase it through the hole in her memory, she—

Pressure against her neck, a soft hiss blooming under her ear, then cold spreading through her veins, taking the sliver of sight, the pain, the...

Time fractured.

She dreamed.

It didn't hurt in the dream and warmth suffused her bones from the fire in the long, low grate along the wall. The delicate strains of a flute teased her ears, the quiet, lilting melody high and sweet. Pale light from the quarter-moon swept through the glass overhead, enough light to silver the pale wood floor and cast long shadows from the heavy steelcrete beams supporting the ceiling. She stood in that space and breathed in calm along with the soothing scent of sandalwood, the crackle of the fire and tried to forget the bitter aftertaste of death.

Her hands were dirty, the creases crusted with blood, the nails ragged and torn. She put that blood-stained hand to the corset-like belt holding her overrobe together, felt the almost-sigh as the nano-seams parted at her touch, the nanite-reinforced armour falling to the ground. The sword went with it, clattering as it hit the wood.

She left them there, gliding across the fire and moon-lit room on silent feet. She shed the overrobe as she went, pushing it off her shoulders to puddle on the floor, a pool of black silk spilling across the wood. It would have to be discarded, too many rips and slashes, too much blood for the delicate fabric to be repaired. Her inner robe went next, the soft fabric a crimson river trailing in her wake, leaving just nanoarmour to flow over her skin. It hugged every curve and line of her body, drinking the light and refusing to let it go until she was just a human-shaped shadow.

From the chin down, she was visible only in her absence, a being made of the void, silent and deadly.

A door—an unadorned, hard-edged rectangle cut into rough rock—shushed open.

She stepped through.

The door whispered closed.

The moonlight followed her, streaming through window and transparent ceiling, silvering the rock-hewn wall on the other side, leeching it of warmth. But then there was no warmth to be had here, even when the sun was high. No fire to crackle and waver, no gentle music to grace the ear and take away the screams, just the cold, snow-topped mountains and white-coated firs, an ocean of spears pointing to the night. The mountain palace's enviros kept the cold out, the nanites running through the triple-paned plas-glas and marble-wood floors, regulating the temperature down to the square centimetres under her bare feet, but still... That chill reached through every nano-metre of technology and lodged in her bones.

She padded down the corridor, under more thick concrete beams, bare feet silent on the wood.

Another door waited at the end. The ancient, blackened timbers shushed aside like the first, but instead of cold, warmth spilled from the doorway, golden light and the twitter of birds, the scent of roses rising with it.

She hesitated before she passed the threshold, a nanosecond where her foot hovered, her muscles froze and her heart stuttered. Just a nanosecond, barely long enough for even the palace AI to notice, but an eternity to the timeworn woman on the other side.

The Ancient One lifted her gaze. The void had more warmth, more humanity, more compassion than the pit-dark eyes in the wizened bronze face. The soul that stared out of it was centuries past its due, had seen wars rage and planets die, had inhabited a hundred faces and was old only in memory.

The ash-white hair spilling over the Ancient's shoulders did nothing to soften her, neither did the richly painted lips, the sumptuous folds of her carefully chosen robes, the gleam of silk, the way she sat on the divan.

Not even the sunlight trickling through the soft petals of the cherry blossom that spread its branches over her head, the warm golden rays carefully simulated to waver just so. The tree itself rose out of a mound of manicured grass, its long, spindly arms covered in delicate pink blooms that fluttered to the ground around the Ancient One. But never on her.

Du'ata's foot met the floor, carried her over the threshold.

The door closed behind her as silently as it had opened. As the warmth and light closed around her, as the sweet bird song twisted through her ears and the sweeter scent of blossoms reached through her nose to stick to her tongue, she wished for the snow, the firs and the swell of the flute.

She padded across the sea of gleaming wood.

The Ancient One watched.

There was no sign, no signal, but Du'ata stopped, frozen solid by a twitch of the Ancient One's eyelid.

She did not breathe.

The Ancient One stared, the cold, fathomless gaze boring into her core, or maybe it was already in her core, in the clean, empty space in her memories.

The Ancient spoke. 'You are not here. You are there.' The words, deep and calm, came from everywhere and nowhere, rising out of the air itself, seeming to echo off the walls.

An image played like a mirage on the back of Du'ata's lids. Herself, up to her neck in a regen tank, a brace supporting her head while the rest of her floated supine in brilliant blue fluid. Around her, the tight confines of a small shipboard med bay, the white bulkheads and deck-plating softened by the dim lights and the hush of air cyclers.

The Ancient spoke again, voice rising from that dark, empty space, filling her bones with cold. 'They are there.'

New images, faces made fuzzy by the view through shuttered lashes, the angle of her head on the supporting headrest, the sticky remnants of pain and injury. A woman in dark armour, short and lithe, a long braid reaching for her waist. Beside her, a man with a slim, deadly sword attached to his back.

She recognised him, the neon green flecks in his hair—why go grey when you can go neon, he would say—the slight hitch in his left shoulder, like the sword hilt poking over it might hit him in the eye. It never did, never could. That slight hitch, the faint wrinkles at the corners of his yellow eyes, the way he shuffled when he walked—deliberately, mind you—had saved their lives many times, made many underestimate the wily strength and speed in those old, weathered limbs.

Rehc. Rehc was there and beside him…

A woman in ship robes to rival the Ancient's, but pearly white, the material shining with embroidery and the fainter shimmer of nano-weave. Her long red hair bound in intricate braids atop her head, the tall weedy teen at her side a carbon copy of their mother. She knew those figures too.

'You are not done yet.' The words belonged to the Ancient. 'Get up.'

She tried, commanded arms to rise, legs to brace, stomach to tense, but nothing happened.

'I can't.'

'You can.' The Ancient rose, no longer solid, the divan turning to smoke under her, the cherry tree at her back fading, leaving just the golden, manufactured sunlight and the void in the old one's gaze. 'Rise, Terrashar.' Her voice deepened, echoing through the dream. 'Rise!'

The command reverberated in the empty space in Du'ata's brain, filled her bones, her muscles, her skin. Everything was alive, the blue regen fluid blinding in its vibrancy, it's tinny sweetness thick on her tongue, filling her nose. And with that vibrancy, that brilliance, came the pain, the fire under skin, the lightning under torn fingertips, the spears from shattered bones and sliced tendons.

Muscles that had refused to move, nerves that had stoppered her will, bunched. Pushed.

In the dream, she rose. In the tank, in the real, she—

There was a disconnect, a schism as part of her, the part behind her eyes with the Ancient's command ringing through her skull, rose from the tank, regen fluid sheeting off her shoulders, sticking her hair to her naked back. The other part rolled its head and struggled to twitch a finger.

Alarms screamed and lights flashed around the tank. In the dream, the alarms pierced her ears, strident and piercing, and in the real...

Joy warmed the Lady's face, and the woman in black was moving. Flowing across the grey-white med-bay, a piece of the dark, like Du'ata had been. In the dream, slicked in her own nanoarmour. But not now. Not now.

Naked and cold and feeble, flesh wrinkled like an old, white prune. No strength in her bones, no steel in her muscles, not even enough breath in her lungs to scream as all that pain cracked and splintered under her skin, in her muscles, through her bones.

In the dream, she stood stooped and shivering, regen fluid sloshing around her knees, unsure if she could raise them high enough to step out of the tub. And in the real... in the real, she watched the woman in black coming for her, braid swinging with every step, a chill, gliding menace in every move.

And Du'ata with nothing, except for the Ancient, except for the old one's words echoing in the empty space.

And the nanites floating in the tank, in her blood, repairing tissue, mending bone, swimming in the dark empty space with the Ancient.

Except for that.

The woman was at the tank, and somehow she was both standing and kneeling. Her gaze weighed on Du'ata, heavy and insistent, but no matter if the woman was standing or kneeling, no matter if the dream was real or the real was a dream, she was close, only centimetres of air and armour between them.

The Ancient's breath brushed her cheekbone, cold and dry. 'Do your duty, Terrashar.'

In the dream the strike has hard and fast; one moment her hand at her side, the next blue regen fluid ripping up her torso, nanites condensing, hardening, forming a sharp, deadly tip in her palm now buried against the woman's chest.

In the real... She blacked out for a moment, or many, it was hard to tell but when she came to, her palm was still buried against the woman's chest, but the woman was gripping it. Holding her wrist in place.

The blue, watery blade was sunk through the armour like it wasn't there and other liquid, red and hot, was sticking to her hand. Her blood, the woman's blood, mixing and twisting, flowing from one body to the other, and suddenly she was flowing with it and...

...and she was kneeling beside the tank, holding a woman's worn, pale hand to her chest, regen fluid falling through her fingers. Was she still dreaming? Was this all a hallucination and the Ancient and Rehc and Lady.... They were all figments? Had the ImpMits got into her brain? Were they still in her brain?

'Dua.' A man's voice against her cheek, warm breath against her ear. 'Rise,' he said, and there was that disconnect again, as the Ancient's resonant, commanding tones mixed with his.

Rise.

Rise.

'Rise,' whispered the Ancient.

⁓

Time reformed.

'Hello, Du'ata.'

The tall, willowy woman pressed the blade harder against Du'ata's throat.

The golden sword was razor-sharp and somehow warm as it glided over her carotid to rest under her chin, tilting her gaze to meet the other's.

Du'ata's grip spasmed on the jammed riffle.

Flames danced in Varya's eyes, their molten bronze glowing from under the deep cowl of her heavily embroidered robe, scorching her cheeks like an oil spill, giving the white flesh a pearlescent sheen. Her long red hair spilled from within that hood, two bloody rivers lying heavy on the nanosilks's midnight-blue front.

Varya stood, booted feet firmly planted on the deck, head up, shoulders back and the sword steady and true in her black-gloved grip. No expression marked her face—no sneer, no satisfaction, no conflicting passions or loyalty—but Du'ata felt the heat from the other woman's eyes, the flames of victory licking her skin, barely contained by Varya's flesh.

'Varya.' The name burned Du'ata's tongue, made her insides

twist, and sucked every inch of warmth from her bones. 'The Ancient sent me.'

'Mmm.' The sword bit into Du'ata's flesh. 'Yes.'

Pressure under her chin, the nanosteel commanding her to rise or lose the few slim threads of hope she had. So long as she wasn't dead, there was a chance for Rehc and the Lady to escape, all she had to do was keep Varya's attention—

The sharp *clunk* of massive deadbolts retracting vibrated through the deck, and the emergency airlock, not blown in by the ImpMit soldiers, cycled open.

The airlock Rehc and the Lady had escaped through.

Du'ata's gut made another twist.

A head was tossed through the opening, black and neon green hair tumbling through the air, landing with a wet, meaty thwack. It rolled a few more times, blood a brilliant red trailing in its wake, its coppery stench filling the air, before it came to a stop at her feet.

Rehc stared at her.

Bile touched Du'ata's tongue, hot and bitter, before she swallowed it down.

She didn't look to the airlock, didn't want to see if another corpse or another head would tumble through, didn't need to know if the Lady and her daughter were alive or not.

Not yet. Not now. If she did not make it out of this, it would not matter if the whole universe died.

You are here.

Back still pressed to the bulkhead, Varya's sword following every twitch, Du'ata rose, hand locked around the half-forgotten rifle.

They are here.

A smile flirted with the corner of Varya's full, dusk-pink lips. Behind Varya, gliding through the open airlock like a slice of darkness, Rehc's naked sword in his hand, came a man in black.

Rise, Terrashar.

'The Ancient sent me,' Du'ata said again. She glanced to the man, stared at herself in the shiny black mask – long blonde strands of hair stuck to her cheeks and jaw by blood and sweat.

There was a tension in his shoulders, a kind of weight that compressed the air between them.

She looked away, back at Varya's burning eyes. Varya's blade took another bite of flesh as she spoke. 'Both of us, Rehc and I.'

Jealousy spoiled the satisfaction curling Varya's lips, the blade making another kiss. 'Rehc died for you, sister.'

Her attention slid over Varya's shoulder, the blood-hair spilling down her chest, back to the man and the sword in his hand.

Du'ata's hand ached for the weight of her own sword, the shifting, black-lacquered hilt, the nanite-enhanced fizz as it connected to her nervous system. Its strength and promise sliding through her muscles, as much a part of her as her bones, as Rehc's sword had been part of him.

'That's not yours,' she said to the man.

He didn't speak, didn't move, only that weight, that tension shifted, grew heavier, and somewhere, deep in the yawning pit in her memory, something monstrous flexed sleeping muscles.

Rise.

Blood and blade and muscle.

Blue regen fluid responding to her command, to nanites in her body, coiling up her arm, a dagger forming in her palm. The tip sinking through armour and flesh, the woman holding it there, a voice whispering in her ear.

'*Rise.*'

Du'ata's blood on Varya's blade, the nanites infused into the haemoglobin infecting the sword. The sword as much a part of Varya as Du'ata's was of her, as Rehc's had been of him, part of her nervous system. Her muscles. Her mind.

For a second, a moment within a moment, time stopped, stretched, turned elastic and sticky. The sword was a highway, a superconductor down which Du'ata raced, and gripped and held, *commanded* Varya's muscles to stillness.

Varya's molten gaze widened, panic bringing out the oil spill across her cheekbones, standing out as her face lost what little colour it had.

The man in black moved, a shadow, Rehc's sword raised, the green-stroked blade cutting the very air, making it scream.

Twisting away from the blade at her throat, breaking her hold on Varya as she did. The rifle was warm in Du'ata's grip as she raised it in two hands, finger finding the trigger.

Phzt, phzt, phzt.

The man stumbled, black nanoarmour absorbing the first two hits, rifle pulses dissipating across his chest in bright electric waves, but the third... the third went through. The nanoarmour over his stomach shattered, blood spilled, the greasy scent of burnt flesh filling the air.

No time to worry if he was out, if the solider's chem-pharm was already pumping him full of adrenaline, keeping him moving, because Varya was coming.

Rage twisted her face, turned those lush, dusk-pink lips to a teeth-baring snarl, the pearlescent sheen to a scar across her cheeks.

The golden blade was coming down, nanites—Varya's nanites—running through the steel, turning the edge the same molten bronze as the woman's eyes.

No time to dodge, barely enough to shove the rifle between them, useless as it was with that bulkhead-melting sword aimed at her throat. Varya's blade would pass through it like butter, clean and soft and easy.

A different blade—Rehc's blade, the edge eye-searing green— severed Varya's hand.

The other woman fell, head separated from shoulders, another bright red arc painting the bulkhead and Du'ata's face.

Behind her, the man still stood, but not for much longer if the tremble in his knees and the hunch to his shoulder told the tale.

The rifle came up, pointed at the shiny black mask. Her finger tightened on the trigger. Froze.

She should kill him. Kill him for killing Rehc, kill him so there was one less enemy at her back, hunting the Lady down, making her spine itch.

She should kill him, but her finger… Her finger was stuck, her gaze caught on that hunched shoulder, the way he shuffled backwards, hit the bulkhead and let his legs go out from underneath him.

The thing in her mind stirred.

Rise.

The man slumped against the grey-white wall, blood darkening the hole in his armour, nanites already filling in the fist-sized hole over his abdomen.

She kicked aside Varya's sword, the golden blade spinning across the deck, Varya's hand still attached, fingers clenched forever around the hilt, and knelt at his side.

'Dua.' Her name came out muffled by the mask, and the monstrous thing in the pit of her memory woke.

In the black shiny surface, her reflection wavered. Long nose and pale white skin of her face morphing, the sharp cheekbones melting, softening, growing small and rounded, eyes bigger, lips fuller, until a different woman peered back at her. A woman who was her, or rather, *had* been her.

Once.

Before the airlock had blown.

Before she bled and died and took a new body. A new face.

Her consciousness a pattern of electrical impulses, her nanites the transmitter, her blade the conduit.

Blood and blade and muscle.

She pulled the man's helmet off. It wasn't Rehc's face, the man's complexion was a pale gold not black, his eyes green instead of yellow with none of the lines drawing crow's feet at the corners, but the smile warming his thin lips was familiar, the nanites in his blood already turning the ink-black hair at his temples neon green.

His head lolled, staring back down the corridor, his neck a little too loose, the muscles weakened by blood loss and pain, the nanites in his system no doubt stretched to breaking. Transmission was difficult, and the wound in his belly would make it doubly so.

'Took you long enough,' he said.

'Shut up.' She picked up his sword, slid it home in the sheath over his shoulder, before leaving him slumped against the bulkhead to fish her own blade out from under a corpse.

The dead woman's face was small and round, with full lips and big, leaf-shaped eyes, just like the ones in the helmet's reflection, except these eyes stared sightlessly at the ceiling. Shrapnel from the blown airlock pierced her chest, a thick, inch-long pierce of scorched and melted steelcrete stuck between her ribs, her red and teal robes dark with coagulated blood, the bum-sweeping braid lifeless on the deck.

Du'ata returned to Rehc, looped his arm over her shoulders and dragged him to his feet.

'Transmission's a bitch,' she said.

CORPSES
&DEMON
HORSES

INTRODUCTION

This is a funny little story that started off with a first line prompt that went somewhere… strange, and unlike the other stories in this collection, you will *not* find it on my science fiction timeline… Unless it's buried somewhere in *I Am Maggie*'s virtual world… Food for thought.

Corpses & Demon Horses is loosely connected to another strange little story, *Little Black Book*, which appeared in the very first *Short Bits* collection, and is inspired by some of the animals in my life.

Dog's love of smelly substances and the missus's disgust at such are reflections of my mum and her dog, while Horse's uppityness comes direct from the antics of my own trusty steed, and Shetty… The small, fluffy pony breed known as the Shetland came by its reputation honestly.

The story was a hoot to write, not only because it's weird, wacky and gross (three of my favourite themes), but also because, as it progressed, I started envisaging a whole new world to go with it. I've even written *another* short story set in the same universe, but you'll have to wait for that one :)

Learn more about the writing of *Corpses & Demons Horses*.
Scan the QR code for the audio commentary.

CORPSES & DEMON HORSES

'What should we do with the body?'

'Niyha's paying good money.'

'For what?'

'The eyes.' Magpie paused, cocked her head in one of those weird, sharp movements that always made Dog's skin crawl. 'The toes.'

He considered the corpse's feet, bloated and purple with death, skin starting to slip from its time in the water. There was still pink polish on the nails, a fat-cheeked feline inked on the bridge of the right foot and a shiny bracelet around the ankle. The rest of the corpse was naked.

Dog sniffed and then wished he hadn't. Not even the milk-rich smell of cow shit or the earthy wet of the river—running brown with the sediment pulled of freshly tilled paddocks, an iridescent chemical stain snaking through it—could cover the stench of rotting flesh.

'I ain't carrying it,' he said. Normally he would, the scent of dead shit made the missus wild, but there were shades of dead, and this one was on the uncomfortable threshold of fresh dead and not-quite-dead enough. Plus, he was pretty sure the stomach was going to pop, either that, or the human'd swallowed a sheep whole just before it died. A squirmy, expanding sheep.

With maggots.

He shuddered just thinking of the scrubbing if he got that shit in his fur or on his shirt. Not just scrubbing but scolding too, and the cold hose. The missus'd probably tie him up on the back of the ute again and drive into town.

To the Dog Wash.

With the Demon Dryer.

The second shudder wracked his spine all the way from the tip of his head to arse, almost popping his tail out of his human flesh.

Magpie shifted, sharp and jerky, still new in her human flesh and awkward with it. The shirt and shorts he'd only just managed to shove on her—if only so the local humans didn't go looney again and the missus stayed off his tail—didn't sit as well as they had when they'd set off from the backyard. It took a little time to settle into human flesh, and Magpie'd done pretty well, but he reckon'd she'd be sprouting wings to go with the feathers in her hair before long.

She flexed her bare feet, black and scaly, just four toes and too-long to fit into any of the human shoes Dog'd had stashed under the porch. At the moment, she was contemplating her own feet and then the corpse's and then her feet again, neck snapping to and fro, and Dog had to look away.

The way the feathers sticking out from under Magpie's white hair kinda *slapped* on her shoulders, like puppy *crack crack cracks*, was too much. Made him think of the sheep hocks the missus had stashed in the bottom of the chest freezer, like he wouldn't scent them out under all that ice-cream and pizza.

'I cannot carry it,' Magpie finally said. 'It is too big for me.'

'No shit,' he muttered. For a bird—and maybe even for a dog, he admitted to himself on occasion—Magpie was pretty bright, but sometimes he wondered if all that time above the ground starved her brain of oxygen.

Even in human flesh, Magpie was a pip-squeak.

Dog crouched beside the corpse; female and young, he thought, although it was hard to tell with its flesh all puffy, straightening out the lines humans tended to get. They weren't many marks on it, and the scent, though enough to ruffle his hackles, didn't carry the sweet tempting sliminess of dog bait.

It was in good condition, and Niyha'd probably pay good bones for more than just its eyes and toes, especially if it was in one piece.

He slapped his knees and rose. 'I'm going to get Horse,' he said, already squelching through the ankle-deep mud toward the house.

'Horse does not like dead things,' Magpie said. 'Remember the sheep?'

Dog stopped, one foot lifted. Yeah, he did. He'd tagged along on one of the missus' and Horse's strolls. The sheep carcass had been pretty ripe, a good few days dead in the sun, the stomach and guts hollowed out—he'd scented Fox on that—perfect for a nice roll. And he'd been doing that, planning a little wash in Horse's trough to rinse the smell off enough the missus wouldn't catch whiff, when Horse'd blundered in.

The uppity fucker had gone sideways, all big-eyed and snorty like he didn't enjoy a good roll in the mud himself, and the missus had landed on her arse.

That had *not* been a good day.

Stupid horse.

He growled, thought about it a second. 'I'll get Cow.'

Magpie clacked her tongue. 'Sun's going down.'

Fuck. Cow'd be lining up for milking, and real irritable too if he tried to pull her out. He rubbed his side. Might even land a kick.

'Goat then,' and he turned back to walk away—

'It was shearing day last week, and you nipped one of her kids in the muster.'

Crap.

'Sheep—' he began and then cut himself off when Magpie cocked her head and gave him a look that made *him* feel stupid. But yeah, he'd earned that one.

Missus'd cornered one of the flock's elders the other day and now most of him was in the freezer, under the ice-cream and pizza. The rest... Dog licked his chops, the elder'd tasted pretty good, a little strong on the back of the palate, but that's how it was with the old ones.

But if Horse and Cow wouldn't come, and Goat and Sheep were mad at him, that just left...

Dog's short russet-brown hair quivered as his human ears slid up his skull and got longer, only to flatten. 'Shetty,' he said. And no, his voice *did not* waver and that was *not* his tail growing out of his arse at just the thought of the shaggy little demon.

Magpie nodded. 'Shetty,' she said back. Firm. Confident without a lick of fear, in the way only a creature that could fly could be. Fly, safe and high out of the reach of the Spotty One's teeth and hooves.

Dog shuddered. 'I ain't getting Shetty.'

He turned from the house, squelched back through the mud, and stood over the bloated corpse. Puffy cheeks, stomach like one of the human balloon things, right before missus added too much air. Just one good jostle and *pop*, except it wouldn't be air bursting out of that stretched white skin, it'd be guts and other gooey things.

Getting in his hair, sliming his skin.

The missus'd go cow-shit.

But there was Niyha and all her bones...

Dog rolled his shoulders, forced his tail back inside his human skin, bent and dragged the corpse's arms over his back.

The Dryer was better than the small demon horse, at least he'd get to stick his muzzle in the wind on the way into town, bark at a few stupid birds, piss on a few tires. Good times.

Better than Shetty.

Anything was better than Shetty.

Felis Fetura

I AM MAGGIE

INTRODUCTION

It's another *I Am Maggie* story!

Just in case you were wondering, *I Am Maggie* takes place around 2056 on the timeline, and yes, it's directly connected to my online serial, *Gamer*. The connection wasn't something I planned; like a lot of my ideas, it happened all on its little lonesome, and it wasn't until I wrote *Scholar* (in *Short Bits Volume 3*) that I twigged to its existence.

Although *Felis Futura* is the fourth instalment in the series, it's the fifth one I wrote, and I highly suspect it might get shunted to fifth place. After finishing up this one, I discovered another little story I want to tell (about the eye under the floor) that will slot in just before it.

Also, look out for Mae and Felix, the main characters in *Felis Futura*, to appear in other stories! I had a hoot writing both; Mae has enough snark to sink a battlecruiser and Felix is the kind of cat I'd want, if robotic self-aware felines were a thing :).

Learn more about the writing of *Felis Fetura*.
Scan the QR code for the audio commentary.

FELIS FETURA

Mae slammed her palms against the cold, slimy concrete and cursed.

She stepped back, the sharp, weed-choked pebbles digging into her soft-soled boots, and looked up at the huge old door with the dragons and tigers carved around the equally massive portholes in its two-storey surface, and swore again.

The fucking thing wouldn't open.

The guts of the control pad lay open on the concrete pillars that supported it, ancient bio-circuits and gel-filled wires trailing down the water- and moss-stained sides. Beyond the overhanging portico, the monsoon turned noon to dusk and made the air sit thick on her skin. She almost couldn't hear herself swear over the rain pounding the curved roof.

After these last few days in the humid hell of Ineron XII's tropic belt, the funky, fetid smell of the hydroponics bay on her little ship would be a fucking delight.

'Fuck.'

'Swearing won't help.' The gravely, fractured voice spoke in her ear, coming through the comms implanted in her jawbone, even though the speaker was above.

'How the fuck do you know?' She punched the slate-grey door again. Mae couldn't even find a fucking *seam*, a single split down the middle or sides to indicate the slab moved. And yet, she knew it did. Knew it because she paid the fucking hacker enough to make sure it did.

'Fuck!' Another fleshy thud. 'Fuck, fuck, fuck!'

'You're going to hurt yourself,' came the lazy drawl from above. And of course, Felix could still fucking drawl even though the previous-level boss had taken out his vocal processor and the only medpacks they had left were the shitty little green ones, barely enough to heal the scrapes on her knuckles.

She glared up at the huge white cat sprawled along the edge of the curving rooftop, like the useless fucking feline he was. 'You could fucking help.'

He swished his tail, the sleek interlocking white plates and ornate silver of his hard-case glistening even in the dull outcast light of the monsoon.

He blinked at her, long and slow. First his inner shutters and then outer. He yawned. 'Why would I do that?'

'"Why would I do that?"' she parroted back. 'Because you're my fucking teammate, you arsehole.'

Another yawn, and this time a stretch, first his forepaws – silver sickle-like claws springing from robotic paws, delicate white whiskers laid against armour-plated muzzle, ears pressed flat to his head; arched his back – the ornate, armoured curves protecting his neck and hunching, the long, sleek spine hollowing all the way down to his hindquarters. More sickle-like claws flashing in the half-light, tail snapping straight and then curling over his back.

Just as slowly, the leopard-bot rose and leapt.

A hundred and seventeen meters straight down, landing on the brain-smashing pebble and stone path like it was a fluffy fucking cloud. Fucking show off.

That's what she got for purchasing a pretty, elf-made bot. All style and fucking attitude.

The snow-white leopard sat, all fancy pearl and silver, head level with her breastbone, and flicked his tail over his toes.

He looked at her.

She looked at him.

'Well?' she said.

'Well, what?'

She hissed. Pointed at the door. 'Are you going to help or what?'

He blinked. Slowly.

She wouldn't growl. She wouldn't.

The long, elegant tail flicked.

No growling. None.

He blinked again and yawned, that long silver tongue curling against the roof of his mouth.

He was doing it to fuck with her, she knew it. She. Knew. It—

He sat back, twisted like a pretzel and washed his raised back leg—

'Oh, for fuck's sake!'

An ear twitched in her direction.

She growled, couldn't help it. The sound burst out of her chest, high and rumbly, cracking on the end.

The leg lowered. The head came around, that flat, delicate muzzle with its inlay of filigreed silver poking her in the chest. A purr vibrated the air between them.

'I love it when you growl like a little squeaky toy,' the big synth-cat said. He stretched, rising on his haunches and rubbed his cheek against hers.

Elf-steel was smooth and cold, diamond wrapped in silk, and Felix's breath smelled of grease and the peculiar sweet, metal tang that came with it. It was nice; sent a little shiver across her back every time the synth-cat got affectionate, not that she'd ever tell him that.

Arsehole probably knew it already.

The fucker.

Mae's lip curled, even as that "little squeaky toy" sound rumbled through her chest again. 'I will end you,' she said.

He purred, butted her chin with his head. 'But you love me.'

'Next sleep cycle,' she said.

Another purr. Another cheek rub.

Another little shiver.

'I'll put your core in the old hound unit,' she finished. 'You can be a dog.'

The purring stopped mid-cheek rub.

The grease and sweet metal smell retreated.

Felix sat back, ears and whiskers flat and stared at her.

She stared back. Blinked.

When Felix snarled, inch-long canines flashed in the dim monsoon light, sickle moons promising retribution. The whole "you wouldn't" was written across his big-eyed feline face, but she would, and the cat knew it.

He stalked past her, disgust in every short, sharp twitch of his tail. One twitch in particular almost taking out her knee, but she dodged it. The plates along Felix's spine ruffled, and there was an extra *skritch* as his claws dug into the flagstones, but he finally stopped in front of the door, sat back on his haunches and smacked one head-sized paw over the gutted control panel.

A hum, short and soft, then electricity arcing blue-white between Felix's whiskers, more of it skipping down his chest, rushing through the silver filigree in his shoulder and into his paw. She knew when he'd made contact with the door's systems when his inner lids half-closed.

Mae crossed her arms and tried to ignore the rain trickling down her poncho's cowl neck as she waited. The door was old, maybe even ancient, in design as well as coding; a relic from the Game's thirteenth expansion that had somehow survived the endless rebuilds and System purges.

Old enough that even Felix's systems, advanced as they were, would have trouble deciphering the code. They could be here for a while.

Mae turned to the jungle and the monsoon, taking in the wide-spreading trees, the scraggly undergrowth – shrubs and fallen branches, orchids clinging to the bark, giant fleshy leaves open to catch the rain, big fat drops that could soak a person clean through in ten seconds flat. She knew. Under the poncho, her orange-fronted shipsuit stuck to her back, while her titanium-weave pants squelched around her knees where they bagged over her field boots. The only thing that wasn't wet were her toes and only because the water hadn't seeped all the way down her socks.

If it weren't for the poncho, hypothermia would have laid her out thirty-eight minutes ago. As it was, the reflection on her HUD showed her lips were a fabulous shade of mauve that'd look just right on a corpse.

Whoever'd programmed the environment here sucked. Weren't jungles meant to be humid?

Not that it mattered.

The dragon had paid her enough to find the McGuffin, upfront too with more promised on delivery. And not just creds, but game time, enough of both to set her up for years, so much that she'd ignored the little shiver of "too good to be true" down her spine.

But then she'd spent a chunk of those creds and more of that time finding this place, trawling through old forums and walkthroughs, peeling apart gossip and rumours and System-myths, tracking all the little kernels that led to this fucked-up little moon with its old-arse door and older-arse coding.

And after she'd found it, she'd spent more time and creds *getting* there.

Enough time and enough creds to make the creepy little shiver disappear.

Until now.

The stroll through the washed-out jungle—leaves more grey than green, like the designers had turned the saturation down—and the ease with which Felix located the cobblestoned path, the lack of monsters and traps (despite the last level boss) shouldn't have made her this uneasy. And yet it did.

Because she was smart.

And paranoid.

And a survivor.

She had the exploit to prove it. Right there, on her character sheet.

// Survivor: Never caught unaware, always with a Plan B. In new environments, your Perception is heightened; threats to your survival make your spidey-senses tingle. Be careful though, not all threats are real.

And standing there, looking out over that washed-out, monsoon-drenched jungle with the ancient, shuttle-sized doors at her back, her spidey-senses tingled. They tingled like a son-of-a-bitch.

'Felix,' she said, switching from audio to the sub-audible comm unit nestled beside her vocal cords. *'How much longer?'*

Text was her only reply. *// Three minutes.*

The tingle, frizzing between her shoulder blades. She slipped a hand under the poncho, reached for the compact little gun strapped to her thigh. The curved, blocky grip was comforting, the barely audible *shruumm*, the little vibration through her pants as it turned on and the new crosshair on the HUD even more so.

'Make it quick,' was all she said.

⌐

Three minutes was an eternity, but just as the skin was crawling off Mae's back, the weight of unseen eyes out in the jungle set to break her bones, the door cracked.

A loud, step-shuddering *thunk* that shook her boots and rocked her balance.

She spun.

Felix was backing up from the door, head up, and a particularly satisfied look on his proud feline face.

There was a split down the middle of the massive rectangle, a brilliant white strip from the upswept roof, through both portholes and into the concrete at her feet. That's what had shaken the ground, unsteadied her. The split travelled not just through the doors but the steps, and as the they opened, the steps slid aside, giant grey plates folding into the pillars holding everything aloft.

Mae stumbled, arms pinwheeling, trying not to get her boots caught in the rapidly disappearing steps as they concertinaed into each other.

The synth-cat was a graceful, white-silver streak leaping from the top step to the cobblestoned path.

Mae tried to follow him down, tripped, automatically tucked her head into her shoulder as she hit the ground and bounced to a stop at Felix's paws.

The ground stopped shuddering.

Rain hit her hard. Fringe plastered to her forehead, little scraggly bits of chestnut brown hair stuck to cheeks and chin, an instant torrent of water rushing over her lips and down the back of the poncho. At least there wasn't mud.

Small mercies.

The tip of the Felix's heavy tail brushed her nose.

She looked up.

He looked down. Rain might have made her look like a drowned warthog, but it turned the cat into a glistening pearl statue, shimmering over the white armour and sparkling in the silver filigree.

Smug, aristocratic superiority hummed in every line of his elf-made body.

Really, it was unfair that a creature without eyebrows could make that expression work.

'Fucking cat,' she whispered.

He purred. 'The door is open.'

She growled and shoved to her feet, cobblestones biting into her palms, fingernails already turning blue. *I noticed* was on the tip of her tongue, but she didn't say it, had already let the growl out. She settled for glaring at the cat, brushing her hands off on her knees before turning.

The door was open in the same fashion Moses had parted the Red Sea. What before had been a massive edifice was a break in the equally massive wall. The giant, dark-grey slabs of concrete hadn't been pushed against the lighter grey pillars, the steps weren't stacked up against the sides. They were gone, leaving just the up-cornered roof and an arch in the wall.

But that wasn't what stole Mae's breath, that pressure was reserved for the slice of greenery beyond the archway. Not the washed out, desaturated green of the jungle, but a brilliant rainbow of green. Deep, rich greens—lime and emerald and jade—all of them clustered beyond the wall, like some force had sucked all of the colour out of the jungle and into the world beyond.

The space between her shoulder blades tingled.

But was it what was behind or what lay in front that made that electric spark jump between vertebrae? Something told her *that* was the important bit.

She shook herself. Important or not, she'd found the ruin, opened the door.

Time to see what was inside.

⟋

A whole heap of nothing, that was what they found. A whole fat lot of diddly squat with a side-serving of rotted parchment, rusty ladles and cracked pottery, surrounded by gunge-filled ponds and a battalion of mosquitos big enough to draw a carriage. Not so much as a suspicious wall hanging or cryptic riddle to give her hope.

Mae slapped at a fat blood sucker trying to work through her poncho. An hour into their initial exploration, she'd made the mistake of shucking the poncho and the even bigger one of pushing her sleeves to the elbow; now welts covered her forearms and the backs of her hands. More climbed her nape and one made a molehill on the crown of her head.

The monsoon had died the moment they stepped over the threshold, though back through the archway, rain still pelted the jungle. Inside the compound, the air was humid, thick, and heavy. Now, it was her sweat rather than rain that stuck her shipsuit to her back.

She pushed an old, wooden trunk over the half-rotten boards of the last building's veranda. The ruin wasn't as large as she expected, not that she was sure what she *had* expected, but after being blinded by the intense green, it had been something more than the square compound with its large, multi-tiered buildings on each side, around a central courtyard.

The courtyard itself was a series of tiered square ponds, they'd probably been filled with orange fish and lilies, as over-saturated as the greenery once, but were now choked with pale bloated corpses and brown, twisted stems. Wooden boardwalks cut the ponds into smaller and smaller squares, partially overgrown with vines and twisted by the trunks of trees and shrubs.

Around the ponds and boardwalks, interconnected wood-panelled pavilions formed the compound's walls, like boxes next to boxes – a single tall, rectangular one in the middle, then smaller cubes spreading wing-like either side.

She'd been through all of them; peered under every sagging sleeping-platform, shrouded in gauzy moth-holed curtains, poked into every corner, every attic, every exposed dust-laden roof beam. She'd bounced on floorboards—put her feet through a few—upturned every vase, unearthed every scroll, torn down every wall hanging. And nothing.

Nada.

Zip.

Zilch.

Bupkis.

Shoving the heavy old trunk onto this last terrace, the box's black metal corners leaving gouges in the soft planks, was a last desperate act. Maybe it would look different out in the sun.

Sprawled over a pale grey boulder, overlooking the largest of the courtyard's grungy, weed-choked ponds, Felix flicked his tail and watched.

'You could help,' she said, feeling like a broken record.

An ear twitched.

Yeah, about what she'd expected.

She slapped another mosquito.

Eighty-six hours after parting the grey, concrete sea, and all Mae had to show for it was the incessant need to scratch and a pile of old scrolls. Some of the scrolls were made of bamboo slats held together with cord, others thick, mildewy papyrus, each covered in ancient symbols that defied her translators. All sixteen of them. Not even Felix's elf-made systems had accomplished more than confirming that the words were an actual language.

And not a bit of it giving off the golden light the dragon said it would.

She finished shoving the trunk to the end of the veranda, popped the lid and stared at the accumulation of nothing inside.

'Fuck.' She kicked the wooden box. 'We've searched everywhere, where the fuck is it?'

Felix yawned, long silver tongue curling. 'Not here,' he said. 'Obviously.'

'The dragon said—'

'The dragon lied.'

She threw a scroll at him. Felix swatted it out of the air.

'He didn't fucking *lie*,' she said. He better not have lied, not with half the credits he'd paid her gone in pursuit of his fucking McGuffin.

'Then where is it?'

'That's what I'm asking *you*.'

'And you expect me to know?'

She snarled at him. 'Well, you know everything else.'

He snarled in return, silver canines flashing, but said nothing.

Mae gave the trunk another kick. The old, mildewy wood—

once a shiny lacquered white with sumptuous apple blossoms and delicate butterflies painted on its surface, now cracked and faded—made a wet *crunch* under the force of her reinforced toe. She kicked it again, her foot going all the way through, up to the ankle. She tried to yank it out, but the rotted wood held on. Another yank, and another. All the time hopping on the other foot, feeling the boards underneath her sag and creak with the impact.

That little tingle shot across her spine.

One more yank and her boot came free, while the other fell through the floor, splintered bits of wood stabbing her ankle.

'*Fuck.*'

'You keep saying that.'

She yanked the newly caught boot out and growled at the cat. 'We need the McGuffin.'

Felix's tail flicked again, a little harder this time, smacking the boulder. 'It's not here.'

She marched across the deck and pointed a finger in the feline's finely chiselled snout. 'It's fucking *here*,' she said. 'And you're going to get off your lazy fucking behind and help me find—'

A sharp, short *frizzle* down her spine.

Mae spun, all her attention on the dank, murky shadows of the last pavilion.

Out the corner of her eye, she saw Felix stiffen.

// *What is it?* the big cat said.

She didn't respond, all her attention on the yawning doors of the pavilion in front of her. The last one, the smallest, tucked into a corner between the sprawling rooms on the compound's south and east sides.

Something was in there.

Something big.

Bad.

Meaner than her.

She activated [Sonic Steps] from her menu bar, took three steps forward.

Waves pulsed from her boots, translucent white circles rushing in every direction – left, right, up, down, around and through. And everything they touched appeared on her HUD, outlined and tagged – height, weight, volume, name, description, threat-level.

Room dividers, lamps, little plinths with bulbous vases and long-withered flowers, a single step leading up to what was once a sleeping-platform. All of it came back as more data to flesh out the isometric map in the corner of her HUD, and if she concentrated on any one thing long enough, more information filled her left eye. But like the rest of the compound, nothing was interesting, nothing came back hot.

So why the tingle?

// *Survivor: ...not everything is real.* The line from the exploit description drifted across her thoughts.

She shook it away.

Her instincts hadn't led her wrong yet. She crept over the threshold, sensing Felix doing the same, a spot of cool comfort at her back.

The pavilion was a single-storey, divided into four separate spaces around a central courtyard filled with the skeleton of an old apple tree, its grey, twisted branches spreading outwards. It hadn't worried her before, but now something about the way the gnarled trunk burst from the weed-choked pebbles at its base, the vibrant, slimy greenness of the moss clinging to the dog-sized stones dotted around the central courtyard, made her skin crawl.

The bad thing was there. In the tree.

[Sonic Steps] filled the main room, *ping ping pinging* with every footfall, reaching the courtyard, adding more detail to the map. Sunbeams filled the room, highlighted the dust in the air, the tattered drapes, the blossoms embroidered on the wall hangings either side of the arch into the courtyard.

Mae paused before the threshold.

Maybe that was why she tasted apples… and maybe it wasn't, said the tingle.

She knelt, pants bunching at the top of her boots, knees brushing the foot-high lintel separating the weed-choked white pebbles from the dank grey floorboards.

Felix sat next to her, tail laid over his paws, languid, relaxed all except for the tip of his tail, the *thwack thwack thwack* on the lintel.

Mae stared around the courtyard. Apart from the tree and the too-neat-to-be-random scattering of slimy green rocks, there was nothing remarkable about it. Open to the sky, enclosed on two sides by sliding doors, the other two by walls punctuated with round, glassless windows. Sun and rain may have soaked the little slice of nature, but she doubted a breeze had ever sighed through the apple's leaves. Birds though...

She thumped the lintel with her fist, [Sonic Steps] shooting outwards.

There was a nest in the tree's dead branches, nestled in finer, thready twigs near the top.

A sweet, high trill sang across her shoulder blades.

'*Did you hear that?*'

// *No.* Another *thwack* of Felix's tail; hard, sharp. Final.

But why?

'*I heard a bird.*'

// *There's nothing living here.*

A mosquito whined beside her ear. She slapped it.

// *Almost nothing,* the cat amended.

But there was. It was in the courtyard. The courtyard she hadn't set foot in, she realised, the only place she hadn't explored.

Because Felix had done it.

Felix had slunk through the little corner pavilion, ears twitching, tail a lazy serpent in his wake. She'd been elbow-deep in the bookcase in the east room, it'd been the eighteenth time she'd uttered the useless words 'You could help!'. The eighteenth time she'd been ignored.

The first rock Felix had leapt atop.

The first one he'd skittered off, his usual graceful self a flurry of uncoordinated paws and lashing white-silver tail.

She'd laughed, enjoyed the satisfaction of the synth-cat's disgruntled hiss, the way he'd stalked a circle around the rock. Like it had bitten him.

Karma, she'd put it down to.

She didn't look at Felix, didn't twitch in his direction, didn't use the HUD to tap into his systems. He'd sense that, like she did the tingle.

The rock though… It was the one on her left, on far side of the tree; long and flat, the perfect spot for a lazy cat to sun himself while his human dug through dusty scrolls and parchment that crumbled at the touch. The slimy green moss wouldn't have bothered him—the benefits of a hardcase over fur—not even enough to loosen his footing. So why had he fallen?

Another fist thump on the lintel.

The map had enough detail to count the pebbles now, to trace the gouges in the pale grey rock.

// *Depth: 3mm.*

The map swung front and centre, taking over the HUD. Nothing in it changed, nothing popped or sparked or glimmered. No monsters sprang from the cobblestones, the tree didn't move, Felix's tail continued its *thwack thwack thwack*. No answers presented themselves, and yet the tingle... Mae shivered.

She changed the perspective, twisting the map until she was looking at it from the top down. Square courtyard, withered old apple tree smack in the middle, five rocks – three round, dog-sized boulders; one wobbly, waist-height column; the flat recliner graced by Felix's claws. Each positioned neatly around it, almost evenly spaced. A pentagram with the tree at its centre, if she so wished.

She tilted her head. Did she wish?

She rose, the tingle still arcing between vertebrae, but something else too, a quiet anticipation brewing in her gut. Or maybe that was the rations she'd almost broken her jaw on, the spicy imitation jerky still lingering. Maybe.

Time to find out.

She stepped over the—

A white-silver flash. Felix getting in the way before her foot even cleared the lintel.

She stared at him.

He stared at her.

'*You found something,*' she said. It wasn't a question.

A tail lash, ears and whiskers flat. He didn't answer.

'*Tell me.*'

He looked away, still not moving.

She went to step left of him—

Felix in the way.

—to the right—

Felix was there.

—rocked back on her heels and jump—

Only to meet three hundred eighty-nine kilos of elf-steel and chased silver, the impact knocking her on her arse.

She stared at him from the floor, disbelief making her dumb.

Felix wasn't Felix anymore, a change had come over him, deeper and more profound than the slick black smoke twisting through his filigreed chest, more terrifying than the tingle hissing and spitting down her spine. More foul than the old-meat stench suddenly filling her nose.

Worse even than the pain of a hundred botched resets or the prospect of corrupting her avatar.

A *thing* flickered around the synth-cat. The HUD said holo-projection, emitted from the lights and diodes embedded in Felix's frame. The horror in her gut echoed the scared whisper in her brain, the one saying—

'Maaaggie.' It came from behind,

She spun on her butt, knees to her chest, hand reaching for the gun strapped to her thigh.

Only the too-green compound, the scummy, translucent water, met her gaze. No red outlines, no monsters slinking over the rotted timbers or swishing through the ponds. No dark clouds creeping past the barrier, just the monsoon turning the sky grey, the jungle with it.

'Maagggieee.'

Breath on her neck, ruffling the short, frizzy strands not stuck to her jaw by sweat.

She scrambled sideways, came up short, caught in the junction of lintel and arch.

Again, nothing. Just Felix and the projection surrounding him, the dark formlessness spreading wings and *reaching*.

It was the wind that moaned that name, the non-existent breeze, or the mosquitoes, the birds in the apple tree... The dead apple tree, bare of leaves. The dank pond, the bloated koi corpses, the rotten timbers and moss.

Death, death and more death.

'There's nothing living here,' Felix had said.

Nothing but the mosquitos keeping the ghost company.

'Fuck.' The forums hadn't said anything about ghosts in this level.

Mae clambered to her feet, keeping well away from Felix and his shadowy wings. Fumbled with the scanner wrapped around her right forearm; poking at the controls. New options appeared on her HUD.

When she'd finally located the ruin's records—the logs detailing its construction, timestamps and signatures marking its birth and development—they'd been corrupted, important logs eaten by time and unsuccessful purges. There'd been no record of its initialisation, no mention of where and when, on which server by which development team, just the location, lost in a tiny sector on an old science fiction server.

Ghosts were nothing more than bundles of random electricity—little knots of code, with or without wireframes—at least on the sci-fi servers, and needed something a little different than [Sonic Steps] to push them into the light. If the rin was an import from a server with swords and fireballs, this wasn't going to work.

Pray for the science, Mae.

Three steps back, toward the entrance, no longer [Sonic Steps] but [Scan] pulsing in the space around her – brilliant blue waves rushing through the room. On the HUD, the map changed again, other shapes joining the white outlines of physical items—the tree and rocks, doors and walls—electronic signatures drawn in brilliant blue. There was her at the centre of the map, arms and chest alight from the gadgets on and in her body. Felix was to her north, a behemoth of power, dark wings lit up with blue veins, and the rest of the room… dark and empty, not so much as a stray network trace—

A blip! Behind her.

She twisted about, took two giant strides around a low square table, back toward the bedroom and— Gone. Fuck it.

Patience, she told the tingle running down her spine. *Patience, just wait for it…*

Another blip, to her left, up the riser and around the dividing screen, the tattered, translucent paper painted with faded koi. Turn right and— Gone again. Nothing but lacquered cabinets decorated with more golden flowers, and a wall behind.

Maybe there was something behind the wall. A hidden room or passageway? A computer of some kind? Was that even possible, on an environment that looked like it belonged somewhere on the mytho-historic servers?

On the HUD, she zoomed the map out. She and Felix became dots, the pavilion a hollowed-out square squished between the larger, more elaborate structures. Symmetrical sides, no unaccounted for lumps or bumps that might have been secret rooms, and the room itself… She stomped her foot, clocked the distances as [Sonic Steps] rushed outwards, compared it to the larger map. The dimensions matched, so why was—

A floorboard moaned behind her.

Breath on her neck.

'Maaaggieee.'

How'd the ghost know the dragon's name?

No one there when she turned, just Felix, half hidden behind the dividing screen, murky dark still writhing through his hardcase.

'Maaggiee.'

And that wasn't creepy at all.

The blip at her side.

She jerked, stumbled over her own boots, caught the old, moth-eaten bed drapes as she went down, fragile fabric ripping. Narrowly avoided braining herself on the frame, gained a few splinters on the floorboards instead as she caught herself on her palms.

The blip again, at her feet now.

She twisted, drew her leg back—

Air. Nothing but dust puffed in the meagre sun from her impact, and a squiggle, a clear space that didn't sparkle like that around it.

She leaned closer.

'You got it for me, Maggie.'

The voice came from the spot of nothing. No… She got on her hands, lowered her face to the boards. They would have been magnificent in their heyday, she could imagine them cherry-dark and glossy, the sweet smell of beeswax rising off the polished wood. Now the red had seeped from the wood, grey creeping in, the oversaturated green from outside sucking their colour along with the shine.

But the whorls and striations weren't what she concentrated on. Once, the floor would have been tightly fitted, the gaps between boards clamped airtight. In places they still were, but not here. Darkness slipped between two boards, less than half a pinky wide, but enough.

She leaned closer. Peered through that little gap.

[Scan] switched back to [Sonic Steps], she knocked on the wood.

Pulses radiated out and down, most of it bouncing back off the floor, a slither making it through the tiny gap and—

Beneath the floor, something knocked back.

The jolt—surprise and fear and a weird, stomach-tightening anticipation—ran all the way to her tailbone.

On the map, a cavity appeared. Two metres down, no telling how many across, not from the thin slice she had.

A deep breath, fear and excitement leaving a metallic taste on her tongue.

Mae knocked again, [Sonic Steps] penetrating a little further, adding detail not just to the cavity but the floorboards, the gaps, the braces, the door under the bed. The hinges on its side.

She scooted to the bed on hands and knees, flopped on her belly, cheek pressed to the floor. Knocked again.

There, outlined in white. The trapdoor.

Breath on her cheek, slipping through the floor.

'Maaggiee.' The whisper came from below, soft, cajoling. 'Where is it Maggie?'

Excitement mixed with acid curdling her gut, made her breathing shallow, added an extra kick to her heart. Not even the sharp, snapping tingle down her spine could dampen it. Seventeen centimetres between the bed frame and the floor. Not even enough to squeeze herself, not even with all air taken out of her lungs, let alone open a trapdoor.

Mae scrambled to her knees, hands braced on the frame. She'd have to push it out of the way.

She heaved.

The frame didn't budge.

Focus on the map, zoom in on the bed – three metres by two point eight, the canopy adding another two in height, the frame made of walnut, the drapes of silk-gauze, weight: one-fifty-six kilos. Too heavy to push by herself.

Felix. She needed Felix.

The synth-cat still sat in the main room, tail wrapped over paws, shadows still twisting through his hardcase, giving him wings.

Hand on the gadgets strapped to her arm, plucking the wand off her bicep by feel alone. Pointing the thin black nano-carbon stick at Felix, the end peeled back, slick black petals folding outward, exposing the brilliant, multi-facetted gem. The scanner's controls one the HUD, [Reset] primed.

The shadows writhed through the silver filigree between the leaves of his hardcase, clinging to the intricate, looping patterns, writhing in the spaces in between. No magic on a sci-fi server, not this deep, this far out. Just energy. She might not know the wavelength or the type, but out in the deep, power was power, and she had a wand for that.

A squeeze.

Power shot through her hand, a thin red bolt leaving the diamond tip, hitting Felix in his beautifully sculpted chest and spreading through the blackened silver. Eating the shadow.

Thirty percent clear.

She bounced on her heels. 'Come on, come on.'

Fifty-eight.

Another bounce, a glance at the bed, at the trapdoor under it. Then at the floor beside it, at the gap between the boards, eyes to a different gap between her feet. Wider, darker. Except for the eye, the bright, bright venomous green eye outlined on her HUD in a gold shimmer.

Breath caught, victory singing through her veins.

The McGuffin.

She grinned. 'Gotch'a.'

The eye blinked, narrowed, then shadowy fingers were pushing through the thin gap, squeezing then stretching. Hooking around the edges, gripping the space between her boots.

The tingle ripping up her nape.

She stamped on the fingers. Hard. Boards sagged beneath the

impact, fibres giving way. For a moment, she thought she'd be fine, that the old rotten wood would hold, and then she was through to her knee. Her thick, knee-high boots protected her calf from the splintered wood, her tough titanium-weave pants her knee.

Still holding the wand, both hands on the floor, the boards a vise around her kneecap, the inky darkness cold on her calf, the eye… The eye…

Lightning sparking off her vertebrae, burnt ozone filling the air.

Wrong wrong wrong.

Fuck fuck fuck.

A glance at Felix.

Eight-two percent. No way was she waiting another twelve for Mr Snarky Pants to help her out.

Mae heaved herself sideways, yanking her leg—

Hands on her ankle, the one lost to the dark.

Cold, cold, cold. Frost ripping through the leather boots, sinking through her skin.

On the HUD, her health falling, status messages boinging.

// Necrotic Grasp. Chill, movement slowed.

Well, hell.

And Felix... Staring straight ahead, the debugger at ninety-eight percent, the shadowy wings flickering.

Ninety-nine.

The hands climbing her calf, tightening around her knee. The chills climbed with them, infecting her torso, her arms, her hands. Fingers becoming ice blocks, elbows freezing.

Ninety-nine.

Ninety-nine.

Fumbling the wand, pointing it with a shaking hand.

Felix moving, Felix looking at her. Relief flooding her system, an additional surge of strength in her arms, heaving herself a little out of the hole.

Felix grinning, mouth open in a cat smile, wings strong and

dark, curling forward, curling *around* her: embracing.

'You got it for me, Maggie.'

She was yanked through the floor.

Letters I'll Never Send

INTRODUCTION

Letters I'll Never Send wasn't meant to be this long. It was, in fact, meant to be less than a thousand words, and well… we can see how well that went.

The inspiration for this one came from two sources: a writing prompt, theme… wait for it… 'Letters I'll never send', for pieces under one-thousand words; and an old-ish TV series called *Veritas: the Quest.*

How the story ties into the writing prompt, it's pretty easy to guess, but for the (short-lived) TV series… that requires an extended stay in my head. Basically, though, I kinda wrote some *Veritas* fan fiction with a character of my own making, and the main character in this is pretty much a spin-off of her. But older and more awesome… and with strange powers.

The chip on her shoulder and her relationship with her correspondent, remains the same but the powers are new as are the mysterious hunters.

Oh, and if you're wondering where this fits on the science fiction timeline… it'd be right up the front, around 2040.

Learn more about the writing of *Letters I'll Never Send.*
Scan the QR code for the audio commentary.

LETTERS I'LL NEVER SEND

He stands with his back to the office, the vaulted ceiling, the heavy dark wood panelling and couch, the desk and the giant lion head embossed in metal above it. He stands there, bathes in the setting dusk and looks out over the city, the skyscrapers piercing the horizon, the residential towers a carpet of brown and grey at his feet.

Many would call this day's end, but his short black hair is still damp and his white shirt and tailored vest still carry the scent of laundry. The coffee in the small green cup cradled in his scarred hand is dark and bitter, and the flat silver rings on his square-tipped fingers with their manicured nails flash in the dying light.

He does not like "mornings", as he thinks of this time of day, he would rather be with the woman in his bed, waking up in other ways. But here he is, and even if he does not like it he can take the moment—the quiet before the chaos begins anew—as the peace it is.

There is little enough to be had.

He raises the coffee to his lips and contemplates the darkening city.

Behind, a door glides open and hard shoes *clack* on the dark cherry floorboards before they're muffled by the Berber rug.

The presence at his back is silent and stoic, waits without fidget as he finishes the coffee and returns the cup to the matching saucer sitting atop an antique sideboard.

'What is it?' He speaks without turning.

Stars pop over the city as the sun falls and electricity takes hold.

A large document envelope is thrust at him. It gleams under the office lights—still dimmed to better witness the coming night—in the way of a sec-package, the tech threading the silk-like plastic affording it a security almost as invincible as the material itself.

He takes it in one hand, the other slipping into his pocket, gaze skimming over his name and ident code on the front, turns the envelope over and stares at the back. Where the sender should be. And wasn't.

A glance up, meeting Gvida's poison-green eyes with a single raised brow, he hefts the envelope.

Gvida shakes his head. 'Sent anonymously through a registered courier. They have no records.'

He considers the envelope, thin and flat, no thicker than a half-centimetre. 'Is it safe?'

'It passed all the scans: no biologicals, no explosives.'

He nods, turns the envelope over again. There are ways to fool the scans, and while there are enough who want him dead to try, few are intelligent enough to succeed, and of those... There were easier ways to get the job done. The woman in his bed is one.

He retreats from the windows, walking between the long square lounges to the desk, pressing his thumb to the envelop's seal as he does. The seal pulses as it reads his print, then a sharp prick as it takes his blood.

In the ten strides it takes him to reach the leather desk chair, the envelope is open and the lights embedded in the ceiling have brightened, turning the office to day even as the city outside sinks to night.

He flicks the envelope open, draws out the sheaf of papers inside, and sits.

He sits for a long time.

Above him, the metallic lion bust—maw large enough to swallow him whole—roars in silence.

The paper is real. Old-fashioned lined paper, the edges yellowed, the grain rough, creases where it has been folded and unfolded in neat, horizontal thirds. There are no intelli-fibres embedded in its surface, no holo-sheen or nano-chips in the corners but it is not the age of it that stalls his brain, not the hotel logo printed at the top or the address half a world away at the bottom. It's the words.

Written in blue ink, the handwriting slanted and almost illegible in places, he's skimmed the first line, and the second, not understanding, impatient to get on with his day and then…

He slumps against the chair back.

There's not enough air in the office; his chest is tight, mouth dry, papers crumpling in his fist.

Gvida hovers on the other side of the wide desk. 'Sir?'

Breathe again.

Dismiss Gvida without looking at him.

'No one disturbs me,' he says.

There is a nod; Gvida always nods, but he doesn't care, he only cares about the letter in his hand.

ONE

[A name is written the top of the page, but it's been crossed out over and over again, until all that's left is a messy black rectangle.]

I'll never send this letter, you'll never see it; I'm not writing it for you, I'm writing it for me, a farewell letter to the girl I used to be.

You should know that before I begin, just like you should know I'm not sorry for leaving, not then, not now.

Did you understand why? Did you care? I mean, I know you cared, but did you care because I was gone or because you lost face when I did?

I could never tell if your feelings for me were real, were for *me* or if they were for Father, to meet his expectations. You made it seem they were for him; the way you'd brush my shoulder, how you'd take my hand. Gently, like you were afraid to get close, as if my half-blood would wash off on you. Or worse, like I was a duty, the mongrel our fathers shackled you to, to tie the clans together and keep you in place.

Then there were the other times, when it was just us and you thought no one would see. Those times made me believe.

Until they didn't.

Did Father make it difficult for you when I ran? Did he summon you to the office, stand you in front of the desk with the blinds all drawn so he was silhouetted by the dusk? Did the sun pour through the window in all those shades of red? Did he stare at you with those cold eyes and try to peel your brain? Did he demand you find me, bring me back and lock me in chains? Did he make you suffer?

Did he?

Sometimes, I wonder. Usually when the nightmares start or the music shakes the floor from the nightclub downstairs; when I can't sleep. I imagine you standing straight and tall, facing Father, pretending like the sun doesn't blind you, that you can actually *see* his face, the anger in his eyes instead of just feeling it. I remember what that felt like, can't forget it; a weight like the sun itself is burning through the window, carving a hole in my chest.

And the times when he wasn't furious... Those are the times that feature in my nightmares, not even the things I've seen or done in the passing years can completely erase those.

It was always better to see his eyes, to know if they matched the sun or if they were cold. Always better to be prepared.

So I imagine how it must have been for you, and I pray he was furious, I pray he yelled and pointed and punched. I pray you left that office with bruises and a split lip, or even a broken jaw, and not something else. I pray he wasn't cold. That you didn't feel time and space seizing in the face of the soul-devouring black hole that is his other emotion.

I know he didn't kill you. I saw you in that little village near the Hanoi border. I was sitting in the dirt, under the banyan tree, hugging a threadbare blanket against the night. You walked right past me, out of place in your custom shoes and suit, your hair swept back in a midnight wave. You looked the way you always looked in public – tall and confident, wearing that expression, the one that said you'd seen the world and found it wanting.

If you'd seen me, would it have changed?

I was afraid you would see. All you had to do was turn your head and lower your chin. It'd only been a year since I ran, and I'd had... difficulties, was hungry and sick and injured, but I hadn't changed that much. Still kept my hair short then, hadn't coloured it, hadn't gotten my first implant, hadn't started wearing the glasses or the ear cuffs, didn't have the bodysuit or the bracers that hide me now.

Maybe it was because I *was* sick—thin, grey even—that you didn't recognise me. You wouldn't have been expecting what I was then, what the months and the fights had made me. You would have been looking for the princess, the little girl who followed you around the compound, the older one who tugged on your shirt, the teen who blushed and just about fainted the first time you kissed her.

I wasn't her by then. The fights made me tougher, meaner, showed me just how much of Father was in me. How much darkness he passed along with the black hair and brown eyes. I see it sometimes, after a job, that soul-sucking oblivion. It scares me.

Maybe now, if I went back, I could stand in front of Father's desk and match him, black hole for black hole. If we did, would Father and I both walk out or would you be left mourning a boss, or a former-lover?

I couldn't stay there, in that house, in the city or anywhere within reach of him. I am not my mother. Maybe if I had been, maybe if I'd had the force of her resolve, the strength of her personality, the resilience, things might have been different.

Maybe. So many maybes.

I didn't want maybes, and so I ran; ran hard and fast and as far as my wits and the little cash I had would take me.

It wasn't far, not at first, but then the fights found me and things... changed.

They changed a lot.

I'm still not coming home, and I'm still not sorry.

I'll never be sorry.

—T

TWO

CJ,

The fights changed me, or rather, they were the catalyst.

Did you trace me there? Did you see the cages, the "dorms" with the bars and padlocks on the outside? Did you see the bunks? Charitable to call them bunks, more like canvas sheets strung against the walls. There were no blankets, no sheets or pillows, not unless you earned them, and even when you did, you still had to keep them.

I was... lucky, I guess. Ma had made sure I could fight, and Father... If it weren't for him, the things he taught even when he hated me, I might not have made it the first week let alone the first month. Or the one after that.

I died in that place, I died a thousand times. Over and over.

After the first few times, dying gets easier, losing little bits of the person you were seems as natural as the sunrise. It's the first death that hurts the most, the one where you lose hope.

That first death almost killed me – dead for real, not just the metaphorical deaths that came later. It was a shank in the hand of my only friend that did it, the handle of an old plastic fork right in my stomach. I almost bled-out on the shit-covered concrete, the cold was in my bones, the dark stealing my vision. I was sad at first, scared. The girl who stabbed me had been my rock, my safety, even if I'd only been a warm body in the way of the new comforts she wanted. The ones I'd earned through pain and violence yet hadn't learned to keep.

I would have them given to her if she'd asked, but she didn't. She took. She stole.

She died, true-dead, on the concrete next to me.

I watched the life go out of her eyes and waited for my turn.

And then I saw you, not the real you. If you'd been there, I wouldn't be here, writing this nonsense on this shitty motel-room pad, knowing I'm never going to send it. I'd be back at the compound, or true-dead in the family crypt – is there really much difference between the two? One is a death of the soul, the other the body.

I'd rather be the latter, even if the former meant being with you.

It was that first death that gave me life. Watching Amelia gasp out her last, the blood bubbling over lips, her mouth gaped like a fish, that was the moment that gave me strength. As her eyes went still and her mouth slack, I shed hope, the last few vestiges of wishful thinking; I killed the silly girl waiting for you to show up, riding in with your suit and Father's men at your back. Every inch the heir to his empire.

If you had, I'd have gone back happily, gratefully, falling all over myself to be out of that place, with those people, and I might never have left.

I'm glad you didn't come. I give *thanks* that you didn't because I was born in that moment.

I dragged myself up off that concrete, I ripped the shirt off Amelia's corpse and stuffed it against the hole she'd made. I washed it myself, bound it myself. I endured the chills and sweats that came after. I died and I came back, different. The first change, the hardest.

The one where I decided, *truly* decided, I wanted to live and living meant doing things that hurt, things that were hard and dark and dirty. It was the first step; the first death of many.

That place was full of death. My second came when I took my first life. I hadn't wanted to. I'd resisted for weeks, climbing the fight ladder from the little exhibition matches, the ones that happened even before the punters came—the bloodthirsty crowd who liked the hollow thunk of fist hitting flesh—to the warmups, before they threw in the paid matches, the ones with the real money.

Ma always told me I had talent, that the fight was engraved on my DNA, bred into my bones and that training only refined it. She was right, but she never spoke to the will, the desire to win, to do violence. To end someone.

I never had that. I *ran* because I didn't have that, because I didn't want to be Father, because I felt his darkness slithering inside me. I didn't want to be him. I wanted to be Ma, noble and pure; it wasn't until later I knew different, that my vision of her was that of a little girl.

The man wasn't the first I'd killed, Amelia had taken that trophy, but she'd been a reflex, an accident almost. I hadn't meant to kill her, she'd stabbed me once, drawn her arm back for the second strike and I'd just... finished it. My chopstick to her jugular. But the second man... he was on the cage floor, shattered knee, fractured rib, crying at the pain, and I'd stared at him, then up at the controllers and the referee pointing his thumb at the ground.

Kill or be killed. That was the law of the fights. The violence and broken bones were the punters' foreplay, death the climax, and they liked nothing better than seeing a virgin pop her cherry.

I crushed his thyroid, stood on it. Felt it go. That little *crunch* under my bare foot.

That was my second death and the beginning of my true self. My journey to the dark.

To Father.

—T

THREE

J,

When I was a girl, I wanted to be like Ma; beautiful, strong and confident, that otherworldly glow around her. You only had to look at her to know there was something special about her, something *different*.

Was that what attracted Father in first place? Did he know what she was then?

You used to tease me about how much I wanted to be her, would laugh when I dressed up in her clothes and stole her makeup. I got you back though, painted your face like a clown and didn't say a word. You didn't know a thing until Ma came home, and she kept a straight face right up until Father...

No one hid things like Ma. She could keep her face straight as a ruler or smile at you even though her heart was breaking. I could always tell though, there'd be a look in her eye, the tears turning them a darker shade of emerald, and then she'd go to her suite, or take one of the cars out of the garage, and cry in silence, where no one else could hear, or see. Except me.

I always knew.

Ma wouldn't close the door on me, like she would on Father or Nan or the other handful of people she considered friends. There were never that many of them, not after Nan died. I guess I took after her in that respect.

I haven't turned out like Ma, not all the way. I'm not beautiful anymore, and while there is strength in my arms and the same power in my veins, I'm lacking in other ways. In compassion. In mercy.

I lost those, right after I abandoned hope.

The fights started that, Father accomplished the rest.

As much as I hate the man, I understand him now, better than I ever would if I'd stayed.

It's funny, isn't it? How I ran to get away from him, from the control he had over my life, and yet... yet I'm here, I'm... this. Me. Father's little mongrel princess all grown up, a chip off the old genetic tree, just not the branch he expected.

He wanted a mini-Ma, a perfect package of grace, intelligence and *power*, someone to tie the families together. Guess he didn't know the real Ma either, or maybe he just thought the killer could be trained out of me; ballet instead of Krav Maga, poetry instead of firearms, literature instead of survival.

Would Ma be proud? Before, I never feared that she would be anything but proud, but now... I'm not like Ma. Ma had boundaries and I... I have conviction. Purpose.

Father has those in spades. Would *he* be proud? Would he approve of me now, or would be still want the little princess?

Useless to wonder, I'm never going back. Never going to see him, not even to spit in his face.

I never knew what Ma was, she didn't tell me. I guess she would have, when the time came, but I wasn't there. I was in Bhutan, in the mountains and snow.

It came on slow, a few strange things at a time – a mirage in the corner of my eye, burnt bark on my tongue, lemons in my nose, the scents and flavours always changing.

A fever had gone through the village I was staying in at the time, and it'd grabbed me hard; I spent days in a sweat, unable to tell hallucinations from dreams, dreams from memories. So when the change started, I thought it was the fever again, coming back for another bite. Except it lasted not days or weeks, but months, and no matter what drugs I took, how many folk remedies or how many rites the witch doctors tried, it only got worse.

I made my way through the mountains starting at ghosts and spitting out tea that'd suddenly turn sour on my tongue. I smelled dogs where I should have smelled dumplings, went to sleep on hammocks that felt like nails. After the second village tried to stone me as witch, I learned to hide it, and I made my way north, looking for answers.

I never thought to call Ma, maybe if I had... but I was scared.

Scared of the way she'd look at me.

I miss Ma, miss her so much. It's a hole in my heart. I could see her, an anonymous note sent to her hotel while she's on one of her trips. All I'd have to do was drop a code word, a day, a time or I'd stand on a corner or under a streetlight as she got out of a car and she'd *know* I was there, with that weird sixth sense she has.

She'd slip away from her guards, we'd meet, hug, cry. Talk, just like we used to.

I could do that, I could have done it any number of times. I've stood on a dozen sidewalks, outside a dozen hotels and *tried* but... There's a worm in my heart, a vicious, poisonous thing that whispers "she won't love you anymore, she'll look at you and her eyes will go straight through, see all the dark, shitty things you've done, and you won't be her daughter anymore. You'll be *his*."

You will tell me that's not true, it's just my imagination, my guilty conscience imagining things, that Ma will always love me. But she doesn't love Father anymore, does she?

— T

Four

[The letter is crumpled, like someone ripped it from the writing pad in a hurry. Bloodstains mar some of the words, including the name at the top, the ink running into the red-brown like it hadn't been dry when the blood hit, making it unreadable. There are the whorls and twists of fingerprints in the marks, matching the line along which it was crumpled.]

Why haven't you married? The families must be pressuring you to secure their fortunes.

There are no shortage of candidates; it's hard to escape them, or you, plastered all over the newsfeeds. Nightclubs, restaurants, boardrooms, that rather memorable shot of you and a blonde in the women's bathroom. It's like a direct feed into my systems, like no matter how many burners I go through, how many idents or phones or network accesses, you're there. Front and centre, reminding me.

Was it me? Did you really take our engagement to heart? Did you *really* believe?

That... makes me sad.

If it is me... get over it. I'm not coming back, not even when you're dead.

I haven't married, just in case you wanted to know.

Why would you want to know?

It doesn't matter, these aren't for you anyway. I don't even know why I keep the letters. I should burn them; isn't the act of writing them meant to be the catharsis? Spilling my guts on a blank page instead of opening my veins a second time. That's what these are meant to be about, and yet... Here I am, carting them around with me from place to place.

I tell myself that's because there are so few, and the envelope is small, shoved right down the bottom of my bag, hidden under the flap, that I forget about them.

It's not true, or not entirely true.

They're always there, just like you're always there, on the feeds in your expensive suits, looking down that long blade of a nose at the world. And no matter how many times I have to run, I always remember the bag.

I always *come back* for the bag.

I shouldn't. It'd be smarter, safer to leave it, let the bastards tear apart the jeans and t-shirts, the holey shocks and the worn shoes. They won't find anything, all the important things are in my head.

Except the letters. But the letters don't matter, right?

I'm good at lying to myself.

Really good.

But you should know that. Or maybe you don't? Maybe that was something I came to later, during that time after the fights but before I became... me. This. Ma's fairytale warrior, twisted by Father's darkness. Maybe.

You remember Ma's stories? The ones about the women clothed in white and gold, who'd stalk the night, hearing the cries of the lonely and helpless, meting out justice for the betrayed and abused? It took me awhile, after the villagers with their stones and the waking dreams, after I realised I wasn't sick, that I was just... different. Like Ma.

It took me awhile, but I realised Ma wasn't telling me bedtime stories, she was telling me about us, about my grandmother, and her mother and so on and so forth all the way back to the first of us. Whatever we are; those of us with Ma's magic.

I haven't found a name for us yet, I've searched—libraries, folk tales, art, history—found traces, but no name. I've come to wonder whether or not there is a name. Did we ever have one, or are we just our mother's daughters and that is that?

It doesn't seem possible, but then, half the things I can do don't seem possible.

I wish I'd seen Ma's powers. I want to know what they look like, what *she* can do and if it's different from what *I* can do. I want to know just how much of Father is in me, how much of my magic he's *twisted*.

Maybe I will. Maybe one of those days when I'm outside her hotel, I'll follow her and I'll watch, far enough away that she won't sense me. I'll know then, and if the light that comes to her fingers is white and gold, well... I'll have my answer.

I told you about my second death, in the fights, when I killed for the first time. Not an accident, but with purpose.

The fights had many more little deaths for me—of kindness, of mercy, of pride—but it wasn't until after, that the third one came.

It wasn't even a new death, more like a return of the first.

At some point in the years after the fights, I'd begun to hope again, even with the villagers and their stones. It wasn't rescue or family I hoped for, it certainly wasn't you in your shining Mercedes with Father's posse at your back. It was for me, that in my soul, despite the things I'd done, the people I'd killed, that I was still good. That Ma would still look at me with pride. And love.

And then I used my power for the first time, *really* used it.

I'd made it to Russia by then. Gone through the Himalayas and the Mongol plains. Buses, trains, hitch-hiking, even a horse once; I took whatever got me closer to that forest in Ma's stories, and when I got there...

The woman who walked through that forest did not wear skirts of white and gold, her footsteps did not toll as the churchyard bell, and they were not cries of gratitude that followed in her wake. I wore hiking boots that left a blister on my big toe, jeans soaked to the knee in mud and the only cries in my wake were that of the crows, coming to feast on the carnage left behind.

That was my third death, when I knew it wasn't Ma in my soul.

It was Father.

—T

FIVE

[The letter is written in grey pencil on foolscap, the page lined and a little yellow. There's a red margin line on the left side with neat punch holes, while the edge is ragged, as if the page was torn from a notebook. The bottom right corner carries a faint brown stain, like someone has wiped dirt off the surface, and a darker stain covers the name at the top, leaving just a 'J' and 't' legible.]

They came for me again. It was close this time. They're getting better at tracking me down, and so they should, after three long years.

They found me— No, correction, they're *after* me because of the thing in the forest, the crows and the blood and the screaming. If I'd known then what I know now... But it wouldn't have made a difference. They'd have come after me eventually, I'd have given myself away, missed a surveillance drone or been slow scrubbing my digital footprint. The only way I'd have been free of them was to be shackled to Father.

Like Ma.

As much as she hates him – and I know she hates him, I see it in the feeds, in every glamour shot, every paparazzi snap, every vid, it's in her eyes. As much as she hates him, she stays because she knows.

If I'd known... well, if I'd known, I'd have known what I was, what I could do and things might have been different right from the start.

Can you imagine Father's reaction to the magic? Can you imagine what he would do with it?

I can. It used to scare me, it *should* scare me, except I've done those things, left entire compounds screaming their sanity away. And that's not even the worst, because once I did those things, the *moment* I twisted my abilities in that direction, I imagined worse things.

I do an impossible thing and... pop, there's the next impossible thing in the front of my brain, just waiting for me to reach for it. It's as if the knowledge is locked in my DNA, and maybe it is, who knows.

There were no textbooks in the forest, no grimoires or wizened women in hidden caves. I'm left to work this shit out on my own. Unless I let the hunters catch me.

I've considered it at a time or two. They came for me, after all, knew enough to keep their distance and stay out of the shadows. If I didn't sleep in fits and starts, they'd have got me the first time, or the second. Hell, even the third. Those first six months after the forest, they came thick and fast.

Men and women in street clothes, a little too clean and not ripe enough to fit in amongst the addicts and whores. The only ones who hadn't known it were the idiots themselves, and the tension had rippled through the neighbourhood like a fucking wave. It was amazing they didn't pick up on it.

There's a burn scar on my back from that night, just another in the collection, it's not even that big – a few inches long, a half-inch wide, flame-shaped of all things. But even though it's not the biggest, or hurt as much, or nearly kill me—although the scent of scorched flesh is one that hangs in my memory; barbecue is no longer a favourite—it's one of the handful I remember most; one of my marks of learning.

I was used to surviving—the fights, the years on my own... Father—but I wasn't used to being hunted. And don't even call what you and Father attempted after I ran "hunting", that was a poor cousin to what these people do. These people are pros; they're patient, smart, wily in ways a fox could only wish. And they learn fucking fast.

Almost as fast as me.

Although, after the last time...

They only have to get lucky once.

They know what I am, know what Ma is and where we came from, *how* we came from it, and they know what I *should* be able to do, and they were ready for it. "Should" being the key word. I'm not sure if I should thank Father for that or curse him anew.

The hunters were after the righteous warrior, a woman in white and gold helping the helpless, and what they found... I think I made it this far, this long because they didn't truly know what they were dealing with. In all our confrontations, I've never left any of them alive, my control over the dark... There was none, not in those first two years, and after that... Well, I thought I'd lost them; I'd moved continents, changed names, IDs, faked my own death and stayed in places not even fit for rats. Stayed so low, for so long... And then I'd settled down, relaxed a little, found a guy who reminded me of—

And that was the kicker. Three years, eight months and seven days. That's how long it took them, how persistent they were. And in that time... They learned some things, the kind of things that made me wonder just where they got their information.

Did some nicely dressed Europeans turn up at the mansion, CJ? Did they ask Father questions? Did they see Ma?

Did they come to you?

I will kill you if you told them. I know it's not fair, not after all this time, not with you not actually *knowing* and yet... Betrayal hits deep, CJ, and stings like a bitch.

But not as much as I do.

Pray I never come back.

– T

Six

CJ,

I'm not sure I can run anymore.

I'm tired, Jon. So tried. It feels like my feet are rooted to rock and my hands... There's so much darkness on my hands, so much blood. I can't get them clean, no matter how much I wash or what lies I comfort myself with.

Maybe if I could sleep... but sleep comes with its own problems. If not nightmares, or the anxiety of the hunters getting closer—always closer—then it's the power itself.

In Ma's fairy tales, the warrior heard the cries of the helpless on the wind, and the way she described them... I always imagined dust motes sailing through sunbeams, or fireflies on a moonless night, something external. Not the constant muttering, the screams and pleading in my head. Is that Father's doing, his contribution to my DNA? Or did Ma lie to me with those fairy tales?

I hope she didn't lie, I hope the things that come for me when I close my eyes are all mine. I hope that for Ma, the messages come to her on sunbeams and fireflies.

I miss Ma. Miss the way she smells, the rich scent of the perfume she likes – does she still like it? I tracked a target through a department store the other day, dodging security even as I cornered the bastard in the men's toilet, and the perfume aisle... Security just about had me there. A mistake I wouldn't have made before, but now...

The darkness drags at me. I just...

The hunters are getting better, closer each time they strike. They're looking for me now, I can feel them stalking the construction site – three men, four women, two in the truck parked just outside the chain-link fence. The ones in the truck have the drones, a merry little squadron of the things buzzing through the buildings.

They haven't found me yet, they're not even sure I'm here. I can tell, feel it inside of me. Not just how far away they are, or the weapons hanging off their belts, but their heartbeats, their *smells*.

All I have to do is breathe and let the dark out.

I've been tucked up in this hole since I took out the bastard in the department store. I prepared for it. The moment his body was discovered, so was I. It's got that way now, the way the dark works, it's hard to disguise it. And I'm tired of disguising it. Tired of hiding.

I'm thinking of letting the hunters win.

Maybe they have answers. They know about Ma and even if they don't know exactly what I am, then they should have a place to start, an idea of what I'm *not*. And maybe, just maybe, I'd finally get some sleep.

I miss sleep.

[There is a line and the ink changes, no longer blue but black. The writing changes with it, still slanted and spiky, but hurried and messy where the previous passages are slower, the spaces between words larger, the loops and whorls bigger.]

I've left the construction site. I let the hunters find me, stood out in the skeleton of that shopping mall and waved at the drone. I even put my hands out wide and knelt when they approached.

I was going to let them take me, going to get the answers and the sleep I needed and then... That fucking whisper. It crept up behind and showed me the things the lead hunter liked to do.

Nasty things, and not just to others, it showed me what he wanted to do to *me*. To Ma. To all the women like us.

He died last.

I took my time.

He did not end well.

I'm still tired. My feet still drag and my hands still ache, but I won't stop, I won't give in.

I need to know more, and to do that, I need to go back to the forest.

That's where the hunters found me, where Ma's tales lead, where the dark first stained my hands. That's where the answers are, and I was a fool to run so far from them.

Who knows, maybe going back will throw the hunters off, maybe it'll give me a few weeks, a month, even a year of breathing space, time to do whatever it is I need to do. Whatever answers the forest holds, something in me says it won't be enough, won't quite *fit*. Whatever I learn there won't be the end, but a start is better than what I have now; guesses, fairytales and violence.

You won't hear from me for a while. I'm going to stop writing these, or at the very stop carting this fucking bag around with me like a security blanket. Tomorrow, I'm going to clean myself up, wash the blood out of my hair, dig the mud from under my fingernails, change into the clothes I took off one of the hunters, and waltz into the first registered courier I see.

If something happens to me, you'll get these letters. I don't know what you'll do with them, I don't care, but I want you to know, even if it's only to make you wish *[the sentence is scratched out, the pen marks thick and deep, almost tearing the lined paper]*.

I hope you don't get these, I hope you're always left wondering what happened to me, whether or not I'm going to pop up when you're old and grey, and make your life interesting.

Pray for me.

—T

SEVEN

[The letter is typed on standard smart paper, the letters black and crisp against the stark white. The timestamp and location embedded in the fibres read from a few days ago, December 26, 11:13pm, Moscow.]

Jon,

I found it, and just like I knew it would all those months ago, it was just the beginning.

The answers the hunters have lead to more questions, more sleepless nights.

I thought I was the darkness, that Father had somehow made me this way but there's more to it, stories Ma didn't tell, reasons why the hunters came after me time and again. I was right when I thought they wouldn't have gone after Ma like they did me, wrong to think that they knew about her, more wrong to assume that it was Father keeping them at bay.

If they'd known about Father…

They know now.

Prepare yourself, CJ. They're coming.

So am I.

—T

DREAD
SPACE

INTRODUCTION

I wrote a Halloween story by accident.

As usual, I started with a prompt, a word count, a vague idea and then let my fingers do the rest. What came out was unexpected and, yes, the ending took even *me* by surprise.

On the timeline, *Dread Space* takes place in the year 2898, between *Transmission* and the universe exploding 'Terramancer', and one-hundred and fifty years after *The Echo* series. I mention *The Echo* because you might notice some similarities between the spaceship in *Dread Space* and the Sisters in *Echo*.

Learn more about the writing of *Dread Space*.
Scan the QR code for the audio commentary.

DREAD SPACE

Deep spacers tell a story of a place with no name. It had one once, you can see the old markings on its hull, but the words are long since gone, scratched and scorched, by time or intention no one knows. Just like no one knows what the thing is, or where it came from, or why it moans.

It doesn't matter if you mute the comms or silence the sensors, the sound comes through the hull, vibrating through the void to sing in the bulkheads.

They say it sounds like wind through a sun-warmed forest at first, the breeze flitting through leaves, twisting around branches. You can almost smell the perfume of spring, taste the first tart strawberries. Peaceful, beautiful even, but the more you listen… the more you listen, the more you hear the voices. It starts out a quiet, alien babble that's *almost* words, but the more you strain to understand them, to prise apart the pieces you *think* you know from the parts that don't make sense…

Yes?

That's when you hear it.

What? What do you hear?

The moan. The ghosts.

Phfft. Ghosts!

Ghosts. Some say it's the memories of the spacers who died in the place, that's it's the fragments of their transmissions, corrupted by power-shorts and time. Others…

...What? What'd they hear?

It wasn't what they heard, it's what they felt, what they *saw*. A presence. Like a shadow in the corner of their eye, watching, reaching out, waiting for them. Like it *needed* them. And worse than the presence is the loneliness – a deep, crushing desperation for another living being. Even when you're surrounded by a hundred different people, when you're held tight in a lover's arms, that loneliness is there, in your heart. There's no escaping it.

The deep spacers say that if you see the shadow, you'll go mad.

...Like Mum?

Yeah, just like Mum.

...I wish she was here.

So do I.

...

The place, it drifts in the dark spaces between solar systems, traveling the forgotten ways of the Interstellar streams. A giant ovoid with a dozen rotating rings, all moving at impossible angles, nearly three kilometers long, and half that wide and tall. It could almost be a space station, except it moves, not that anyone ever sees.

...Is it a ship then?

Maybe. It's too big to be a First ship though, too far out, too old, travelling in the wrong direction and yet it looks like one of those crazy first-gen designs. You know, the ones in the museums, the pictographs carved into the First World towers?

...The ones they called skyscrapers?

Yeah, those. The spacers say the ship is dead, no power, no drive signatures or tachyon trails, no radiation spikes. Yet it moves, never at the same coordinates twice, but there when it's needed, or, at least, that's what the survivors say. If you can call them that. Most don't.

...Mum survived.

Maybe.

Of those that go look for it... most who return didn't find it.

And those that do... They're like Mum, going out into the deep places again and again, spending everything—fortune and sanity—on the search, their last threads of reason all they have to hang on to before they dive one final time into the deep places—

...

It's okay, we got to Mum in time. Uncle Vipin won't let her go anywhere.

...He can't do it forever. [sniffs]. The spacers have tried, entire ship-families have dedicated their lives to saving sibs struck by the madness, drugs and therapy and padded rooms. But none of it works, the mad ones always find a way, and if the spacers can't do it

No one can. But we're not spacers, and we're not giving up, Ratnam. You *know* we're not giving up. We're going to find this thing, and we're going to *make* it let Mum go.

...What if we can't? What if we get inside and...? What's inside?

Death. At least, that's what those who make it out say, if they can still speak. Most can;t, and the ones who can... The deep spacers who can speak, who made it out of that place alive, they call their friends the lucky ones.

They say that what's in there... what's in there is nothing. They say that what's in there is the most beautiful, most horrible thing they ever saw, that they ever will see. They say the corridors are filled with light and colour, the bulkheads carved with pictures of such exquisite detail they almost seem to move. They say their fellows lost themselves in the delicate dance of line on line, the intricate patterns and whorls. They say friends, family, lovers and enemies never wanted to leave, and when they tried to force them...

...What?

They died. Bashed their heads against the bulkheads. They said there are old, brown-red stains all over the pale-grey bulkheads, scraps of cloth and fragments of bone piled in the corners of every corridor, every room.

The very air is meant to shiver with the sound of their cries, that even with the enviros running a chill races across your flesh, goosebumps marching in its wake, not because of the cold, but the voices. They say it smells of whatever you hold most dear—memories of home, of loved ones, of victories or defeats—whatever scent leaves a knot in your heart, the air is thick with it.

…Why are you telling me this?

Didn't you ask?

No.

…Oh.

Ratnam?

Hmm?

Where's Uncle Vipin? Where's the crew?

We left them behind.

Why?

Because they tried to stop us.

From what?

From going to the place.

Which place?

That place. *This* place.

DON'T MISS
ANOTHER BOOK!

I love keeping in touch with my readers, it's the second-best thing about being a writer (writing being the first best). Every fortnight (or thereabouts), I send out a newsletter with details about upcoming offers, new releases and extra special projects.

If you sign up for the mailing you'll receive exclusive behind-the-scenes extras, such as:

- free short stories
- deleted and alternate scenes from my books
- previews of upcoming books
- pancakes
- quizes
- and much, much more!

Scan the QR code or visit the link below to sign up.

belindacrawford.com/newsletter

Ready for more?

A dark new urban fantasy filled with reincarnated superheroines, inter-dimensional demons and immortal enemies.

Byrne Davin has lived many lives, from noblewoman to pioneer to slave, all of them filled with blood and death, all ending in pain and betrayal. This life, she would like to live in peace, or if not peace then to at least finish high school, maybe even meet a cute guy, go on a date, kick demon arse and be home in time to do her homework.

But she can't always get what she wants, not with an ancient, battle-crazed warrior sharing her soul, or fragmented dreams of an unseen enemy that threatens not just her existence, but that of her reincarnated sisters.

Sisters who doubt Byrne's every word and hold terrible secrets of their own.

A darkness is coming, a bitter cold rising from the depths of the universe on the ravening howl of a bloodthirsty demon horde. And the only thing standing between it and victory are Byrne, her sisters and the lies tearing them apart.

Available now
belindacrawford.com/DemonsBattleskirts

ABOUT THE AUTHOR

Physics makes Belinda's brain hurt, while quadratics cause her eyes to cross and any mention of probability equations will have her running for the door. Nonetheless, she loves watching documentaries about the natural world, biology, space, history and technology.

She's also a sucker for a fast horse, a faster computer and superhero movies. When she's not doing the horse, computer or superhero thing, Belinda writes sci-fi and fantasy for readers who like their fiction action-packed, with diverse characters, butt-kicking heroines and complex worlds.

As a certified crazy horse person, when she's not wrangling six-legged dynamos on the page, she's wrangling four-legged powder-kegs in the paddock. Belinda brings that same certified craziness to her writing with the kind of unexpected twists that'll keep you guessing.

You can keep in touch with Belinda, or just pick her brains about sci-fi via her website, Facebook or by sending her an email (she loves email).

www.belindacrawford.com
belinda@belindacrawford.com

Have news delivered straight to your inbox
via her mailing list. Sign up at:
belindacrawford.com/newsletter